GROWING UP IN
AFRICA

THE TRUE ADVENTURES OF
TWO AMERICAN CHILDREN
IN THE WILDS OF AFRICA

Life is an adventure!
Les Nuckolls
Jenny Nuckolls

GROWING UP IN
AFRICA

THE TRUE ADVENTURES OF
TWO AMERICAN CHILDREN
IN THE WILDS OF AFRICA

By
Les and Genny Nuckolls

Council Press
Springville, Utah

ISBN-13: 978-1-59955-047-3

Published by Council Press, an imprint of Cedar Fort, Inc., 2373 W. 700 S., Springville, UT, 84663
Distributed by Cedar Fort, Inc., www.cedarfort.com

LIBRARY OF CONGRESS CATALOGING-IN-PUBLICATION DATA

Nuckolls, Les, 1931–
  Growing up in Africa / Les and Genny Nuckolls.
    p. cm.
  ISBN-13: 978-1-59955-047-3
  1. Family 2. Africa 3. Domestic I. Nuckolls, Genny, 1946– II. Title.
  PS3614.U83G76 2007
  813'.6--dc22

                            2007013381

Cover design by Nicole Williams
Cover design © 2007 by Lyle Mortimer
Edited and typeset by Kimiko M. Hammari

Printed in the United States of America

10 9 8 7 6 5 4 3 2 1

Printed on acid-free paper

DEDICATION

We would like to dedicate this book to
Sheri and Kari,
and to all of the students,
staff, and parents
of the Dry Creek School District
who encouraged us to write it.

CONTENTS

PROLOGUE

We were living an ordinary life in California when, in what seemed like a flash, we were surrounded by forest, savanna, and a world of wild creatures. We had moved to the African wilderness, and our little house stood beside a dirt road a thousand miles from nowhere. The only things familiar to me were the members of my family.

Dad had accepted a teaching job at an African college. It was located near a small town called Kitwe, which means "skull of the elephant" in the local language. Apparently, in the old days, traders passing through this part of Africa used the ancient sun-bleached skull as a landmark in their travels.

My name is Alicia. I'm thirteen, and my sister Annie is eleven. We have had many wonderful adventures growing up in Africa, and we'd like to share some of them with you. Many of our experiences have been very funny, but there were a few that could have had deadly endings.

Annie is sort of the family comedian with her short red hair and quick wit. I have long blonde hair, and I'm a little more serious, probably because I'm older and wiser. Mom is a lot like me, and Dad is a fun-loving guy who is

ready to hit the road at the drop of a hat.

So, Annie and I will probably tell you most of our stories, but we'll let Dad share a few too, since he brought us here in the first place.

LOVABLE LOUIE

It was a bright, sunny morning as I sat on my bed and looked out the window. There's a small acacia tree in the yard, and I thought I saw something hanging between two branches. "Annie, come here. I think there's an animal in our tree."

My little sister came running. "Where? What is it?" she asked excitedly.

"There. See it? Something long and green is hanging there. It's the same color as the leaves," I replied. We watched intently as the leaves shimmered in the sunlight. The thing we were watching was motionless. It was big, about two feet long, and it matched its surroundings perfectly.

"Alicia, look, it's moving," Annie whispered. We continued to focus on it until we were able to make out a head and a long tail. Our strange visitor firmly grasped the tree limb with four little hand-like feet.

Swoop. That was the sound we heard as a long, foamy tongue shot out of the creature's mouth and caught a hapless fly.

"Wow! Did you see that?" Annie shouted. "Did you see how long that tongue is?"

We watched, fascinated, as the green tree climber captured

flies and insects with its long, sticky tongue. When Dad came home for lunch, we told him about the mystery guest in our little acacia tree. He looked out the window with us until he exclaimed, "There he is! Now I see him. Let's go catch him!"

We stood under the tree and watched while Dad reached up into its branches and grasped the reptile around its middle. With his other hand, he gently pried loose its strong fingers that held onto the small branches. Then he lowered the giant chameleon down from its lofty perch. The big guy was already shedding his green hue, changing his skin color to match Dad's tan hands and arms.

"Will you look at the size of him!" he exclaimed. "He must weigh at least two pounds." Back home Dad sometimes teased his friends from Texas because they bragged about how big everything was in their state. "Wouldn't the folks in Texas like to see this one," he quipped. We had seen small chameleons in California, but none like this.

We put a dry tree branch in my bedroom and placed the big chameleon on it. We giggled as we watched him make his way up the limb. In a full minute he would only walk two or three steps. His movement was sort of like a dance step. One foot forward, pause and sway. Second foot forward, pause and sway.

Our new friend seemed to like it when we held and petted him. For sure he was a keeper, so we named the gentle guy Louie. We soon learned that the word for chameleon in the local African language was *lufumyumba* (pronounced lou-fum-yum-ba). So, welcome to our home, Louie Lufumyumba.

However, Louie didn't live with us for very long. There weren't enough bugs and flies in our house to keep him busy and well fed. Dad said, "I'll take him over to the school. He can live in my office. There's enough stuff flying around there to feed ten of these guys."

African students came to visit us often. It was obvious that Father was a popular teacher. Even after school he would spend hours in his office talking with students, advising them or just chatting. He enjoyed those times, and they were an important part of his job.

Louie now lived in a very large cage in the corner of Dad's office. There were big open windows, and scores of colorful insects buzzed in and out of the room all day. Occasionally you could hear the swoosh of Louie's long foamy tongue shooting out and snaring another meal. His aim was so accurate that he rarely missed his prey.

One night at dinner Dad said, "I don't know what's wrong. The students have always hung out at my office after school, but in the past two weeks, I haven't had a single visitor. It's really weird!" And so it went. Our very popular father was suddenly being shunned by his students. What had he done?

Another week passed, but still no visitors came. However, Dad's office had fewer flies than any place in the school. Louie was doing his job. When my sister and I visited, we played with him, and he seemed to be one happy camper.

One evening the school's headmaster came to our house for dinner. We call them principals, but in many countries they are considered the head teacher, or headmaster. Dad talked about the mystery of his empty office. No student visitors in weeks. What had he done to offend his students?

"You've done nothing wrong," the man answered. "It's that big tree reptile that you keep in your office. They think he has godlike powers."

What? Louie? Our family sat in stunned silence. He couldn't be talking about our lovable Louie. Our friend who changes colors to match the shade of the blouses we wear? Our big lufumyumba who loves to be picked up and held? He has supernatural powers?

"You know," the headmaster continued, "that many Africans are superstitious. From an early age, children hear tales from their elders and from the village witch doctor. These stories are passed down from generation to generation. The innocent-looking lufumyumba who hangs quietly in the tree all day is revered. Most of our African students have been taught that he has special godly connections. If I were a tribal witch doctor, I would tell you a tale like this:

"In the beginning, the god of the earth called for a meeting. He commanded all of earth's peoples to send a representative to the conference to learn about the gifts and rewards they would receive.

"The earth's peoples lived in faraway lands, so they sent their favorite and most trusted animals to represent them. The people of Europe sent the speeding cheetah. Those living in South America dispatched the fleet-footed antelope. And so it went, and all animals rushed to the meeting to learn about the gifts and wealth their people would receive.

"The people of Africa sent their trusted friend, the honorable lufumyumba. Off it went, doing his strange little slow step. By the time the lumbering fellow reached the world conference, it was nearly over. Many of the good things in life had been given to others, but those speedster animals who got there first were greedy and wanted more gifts and rewards. They continued to argue and fight over who had more, and the god of earth was dismayed.

"Finally the lufumyumba arrived. 'You are late, my friend. Many of the gifts have been granted. Is there anything special that you are seeking for your people?' he asked.

" 'There is nothing special that we seek. My people have happiness and love. They have given me their trust to tell you this. Any small gift that you might send would be cherished.'

"All of the other animal messengers were absolutely

astonished. 'He wants nothing; he won't even lie and cheat to get his fair share,' one exclaimed.

" 'Noble chameleon, you make my heart full. After listening to all of these scoundrels, your righteous words are music to my ears. Thus, you will take home these gifts to the African people—the gifts of quiet peace and prosperous lives. They may not acquire great wealth, but they will live forever with the kind of admiration and respect that honorable people deserve.'

"As I said earlier, this tale is repeated over and over by tribal elders to the village children. This is the truth as your students know it," the headmaster concluded.

The next morning we went to Dad's office. I lifted Louie and stroked his leathery head. He seemed to smile affectionately as he gripped my fingers with his strong hands. We walked the big guy to our house, and Father lifted him gently and placed him on a limb of our little acacia tree. The small limb quivered under his weight as he moved slowly to a higher perch in the tree.

Every day Annie and I go out and talk to Louie. He is difficult to locate sometimes, but we usually find him. He looks happily down at us as he listens to our voices, but occasionally our talks are interrupted by a *swoosh* as he goes about his business.

DID YOU KNOW?

- Chameleons are members of a group of tree-dwelling lizards.
- They are known for their ability to change body color.
- Chameleons have long, slender extendable tongues that they use to catch insects.
- These tree lizards live mostly in Madagascar and in sub-Sahara Africa.
- Their two bulged eyes move independently of each other, allowing them to focus on two separate targets at the same time.

THE BABY ELEPHANT IS
A TROUBLEMAKER

One of the neatest things about living in Africa is being able to go on trips with Dad. When he's not teaching at the college, he visits bush schools to see how they're doing.

It's important to understand that some people in Africa live in cities and small towns, but most live in the "bush." Bush can mean countryside, mountains, savannas, or jungles. I guess I'm saying if you don't reside in town, you live in the bush.

My sister and I were reading when Dad popped through the front door. "How'd you girls like to go on a trip with me up through lake country?"

"Yes!" Annie and I shouted in unison. Then something flashed through my mind, and I asked, "Isn't the lake area kind of rugged? I read that it was really a primitive area with tons of wild animals."

"Right you are, Alicia. However, there are a couple of tribal schools up there that might need a little help. That's my job. Are you guys in or out?"

We were in, and the next morning we were out—out on the road, that is, in a four-wheel vehicle headed for the wilderness. The dawn sky was streaked with red, and the green African fields and meadows smelled fresh and alive.

Dad was in his usual fun-loving mood. Without a doubt, he was the world's biggest teaser.

"Do you want to drive for a while?" he asked my eleven-year-old sister.

Not to be outdone, Annie quipped, "Sure, Dad, but let's wait until the road gets a little rougher."

It wasn't long before she got her wish. She didn't drive, but now the road was dirt and more like a big cow path than anything for cars. We were moving slowly as we approached lake country. Frequent potholes were pounding our vehicle hard.

We had been driving for nearly three hours, and we were about a hundred miles or more from home. "I'm going to stop pretty soon," Dad said. "We need a break, and the car engine is getting hot. I can see a little steam coming from the radiator."

And stop we did, but much sooner than Dad had thought. He had just told us his plan when he abruptly hit the brakes. Forest grew on both sides of us with only our cow path road winding through it. There was a large clearing ahead, and we knew immediately why Dad had slammed on the brakes.

"Wow! Look at them!" he exclaimed. My mouth fell open as I stared. The green hillside in front of us was filled with elephants. The herd grazed in the meadow and munched on branches hanging from the trees. Our little dirt road ran right through the center of that meadow. Our route was blocked; the herd had cut us off.

"Aren't they beautiful?" Mr. Cheerful whispered. Did he ever get upset about anything?

"Yeah, Dad, they're just beautiful. But they're not in a zoo somewhere with moats and fences keeping them in. Look at them! They see us! You'd better start up the car and back down the road," I urged.

The elephants continued to feed quietly, but a large cow and two bulls eyed us warily. The two males were as tall as some of the trees. Their huge ears waved slowly in the African breeze. When they reached up with their long trunks, they could strip foliage from high up in the trees.

One big bull turned toward us, raised his trunk, and trumpeted. The shrill sound echoed down the road and out through the forest. "Not a bad idea, Alicia. I think I will back up a little. That big guy is sending us a warning," Dad whispered.

He had turned off the engine when we stopped to allow the hot motor and radiator to cool a bit. As he turned the key in the ignition, all we heard was a grinding noise. The four-wheel had overheated and would not start.

"Look," Annie said. "A baby is coming toward us!" We had been watching the baby standing near her mother. The big cow had been wary at first, but now she was contentedly feeding on tree limbs. Apparently, the mother was hungry because she was paying no attention to her little one.

The small elephant walked down the dirt road toward us. We sat breathlessly as she approached the car. She was so cute and inquisitive. She looked the vehicle over from one end to the other. Then she noticed steam coming from the hot radiator on the front of the car. Steam. Scalding hot steam! She had never seen that before, and her curiosity got the better of her.

She moved closer to the vehicle and reached out with her baby trunk. When she placed it on the spot where steam puffed from the hot metal radiator, it burned. The baby jerked back and let out a blood-curdling cry. She trumpeted once more, even more loudly. "Mama," she seemed to shout. "Mama, come help me!" the young elephant pleaded.

And come Mama did! The big cow heard her baby's cries for help and left her feeding tree. Trumpeting wildly, she lumbered quickly down the road toward us. She was mad and she meant business.

Dad tried starting the car one more time. Then he said, "Come on girls. Run for it!"

We were out of the vehicle in seconds, racing for our lives down the muddy dirt road. Behind us we could hear the mother bellowing, but we didn't stop to see how close she was.

The three of us were breathing hard when Dad commanded, "Okay, let's stop here for a second and see what's happening." What we witnessed the next few minutes was almost mind blowing. You had to have been there to believe it.

The big cow reached the car and quickly pushed her baby away to a safe distance. Still furious, she returned to the metal monster that was blowing steam from its mouth. It was then that she decided to attack that part of the beast. Turning, she sat on the front of the car, directly on the hot radiator. Her vast weight squashed the entire front end of the vehicle down deep into the muddy road.

We watched wide-eyed. The rear of our car now stood high in the air, while the front end was buried in the ground. None of us was able to speak. We stared as the mother trumpeted again, turning in circles as though she was doing a dance. Obviously, sitting on the hot engine had burned her rear end. This mom was really upset!

The elephant herd had been watching the show from up on the meadow. When the baby cried out, the mother had come to her aid. Now the mother was sending distress calls, and the big bulls were charging down the hill to save her.

We could hear the rumbling, and the ground almost shook as the giant males raced toward our car. "Let's get out of here!" Dad shouted, and we turned and fled. After another hard sprint, we stopped to catch our breaths. Pointing up the road at the wreck that was once our car, Dad said, "Will you look at that!"

I stared as a large male ripped off one of the doors of the four-wheel. Another tore off its steering wheel and then sailed it across the tree tops like a large Frisbee. Soon the last door went crashing into the brush as another bull wrenched off one of the wheels. In less than two minutes, our sturdy off-road vehicle had been reduced to a small pile of scrap.

Annie, Dad, and I walked many miles that afternoon. Finally, we reached a village where we spent the night. With the help of its chief, we got word to our friends at the college, and we were picked up in two days. What an adventure! Thank you, baby elephant!

DID YOU KNOW?

- The long trunk of the elephant is used for breathing, drinking, and reaching for food.
- The African elephant is the largest living land animal.
- An African male elephant can weigh up to 16,500 pounds and stand as high as 13 feet at the shoulder.
- The Indian elephant is smaller and does not have the large ears of its African brother.
- Elephants may live in large herds or in small family units.
- Because of their size, bathing elephants have no fear of crocodiles.

Don't Mess with Our School

I met my new best friend the other day. I was playing hop-scotch outside in the sunshine when she walked up to see what I was doing. I had scratched the hopscotch outline into the red African clay and was just jumping around by myself to pass the time. Her name is Joko, and she lives down our shady road in the same kind of brick housing as my family. She lives there with her mom, dad, and brother, Peter. Her dad teaches at the college, same as my dad.

I asked Joko how old she was, and it turns out she is ten. I was surprised to hear that she is only ten because she is taller than me and I'm eleven already. She is very pretty, with dark brown skin, curly reddish-black hair, and huge brown eyes. She wore a cool cotton flower shift, and I'm going to ask my mom if she can make me one like it.

I started teaching her how to jump and play different games in the clay outline. While we were doing this, I asked about school because I've been wondering what it was going to be like to attend school in Africa. She's going to be in the fifth grade when school starts, and I'll be in the sixth.

"We're very serious about school. Going to school is a privilege, and we work hard to learn all we can. It's also a lot of fun, Annie." As we talked, I could tell school here would be different from California. A lot different.

She told me all about village schools and how the parents of the students actually work together to build the schools. Mud bricks are made for the walls and palm tree branches are cut to make a roof. They even split logs to make desks and seats for the kids.

"When your mom and dad help build your school, you take good care of it," Joko said. She explained that there were no custodians to clean the rooms or yard people to take care of the grounds and play fields. "Each class has a work assignment for the week. Some classes will slash the grass to keep it short so snakes can't hide out. Others will clean the classrooms and bathrooms and carry out trash to burn. When our school needs painting, the students paint it. We take pride in our school and we take good care of it, just like it was our home."

I thought about my school in California and how I just took for granted that it would be built and that there would be other people to take care of it. I also remembered that some kids, some who were always in trouble, marked the outside walls with graffiti, broke windows, or intentionally plugged up toilets. When I told this to Joko she was astonished. "No one would dare do those things here!" she exclaimed. "They would have the students, teachers, and the whole village after them and would be severely punished."

I thought about what Joko had told me. I guess when you build your own school and are responsible for all the upkeep, you're not going to let someone mess with it. But this was so different from school in the States that I wanted to know more. I asked, "Tell me about what happens to a student when she first starts school here. What if I were just starting first grade?"

"When a child enters first grade, she is given a set of lined notebooks. One notebook is for each subject. For example, when math is taught, she writes down the problems in the math notebook. She does the same for each subject, such as language arts, social studies, or spelling. The only other supplies the first grader is given are a pencil and a razor blade."

"A razor blade!" I exclaimed. "A little six-year-old kid is given a razor blade? In my country they aren't even allowed to have sharp scissors!"

"It's not a problem here. Kids are taught very early how to use tools, and that includes tools that are sharp. The first grader will use the blade to sharpen her pencil when needed. The blade will lay on her desk the entire school year. She knows how to use it and how to be careful with it," Joko added.

"Students are taught to be polite and quiet at all times. They never speak unless they are asked to by their teacher. When the teacher walks into the classroom first thing in the morning, all the students spring to their feet and shout, 'Good morning, sir.' "

Holy cow! I gulped. This is going to be so different. I started worrying even more and asked, "Well, what about the higher grades? What's going to be happening in my sixth grade classroom?" Joko informed me that grades one through six are pretty much the same: pencil, notebooks, and a razor blade. "Only the work gets much harder as you go along," she said.

"Since there are no textbooks," Joko continued, "African students create their own by writing down as much as they can of what the teacher writes on the chalkboard. By the time a student finishes sixth grade, she will have many of those little notebooks with the pages all filled.

"We carefully preserve the notebooks at home because they will become our life library. For example, suppose a young person is asked to plant several thousand yams on four different-sized plots of land. The former student can always go to her little life library and get help from her math books on how to measure the acreage and how many yams to plant on each plot of ground. Or suppose I want to travel to another part of my country to visit my cousins. I can look at a map in my life library to see how far I have to travel.

"Students here keep and protect their life libraries forever. These little notebooks are sometimes more valuable to us than cattle or sheep," she concluded.

By the time I had finished teaching Joko to play hopscotch, she had taught me so much about my new school that my head was swimming. It was difficult to understand everything she had told me, and I would have to start carefully practicing with a razor blade. But I already had a new friend, and I knew I was at the beginning of a great adventure!

DID YOU KNOW?

- In Africa, school only goes through the sixth grade. Students then take the 11+ exam, and if they pass the test, they can go on to higher grades. If they fail the exam, they go back to their villages to work.
- The school year in most parts of Africa is from October to June and stops during the hot summer months.
- Teachers are highly regarded in African cultures. They have finished the eighth grade and go on to additional education at a teacher's training college.
- Usually there is one teacher for each grade level, and he teaches all subjects. There is also a headmaster (principal), who is a very experienced teacher.
- Most bush schools are usually built by the parents of the students. Classrooms have dirt floors with large shuttered windows.
- The teachers have materials and guide-books from their teacher training classes, but no equipment other than chalk and a chalkboard.

WAFITA, THE
LITTLE BLACK ONE

It was late at night, and the black African sky was angry. Lightning strikes crashed down at our small houses nestled along the dirt road. A brilliant flash appeared in our backyards as yet another clap of thunder rolled through the valley. Then all the lights went out. Our neighborhood at the edge of the jungle was cast into total darkness.

Mike and his family lived in the last house on our little dirt road. They were from Scotland, and he was the college chaplain. He led church services every Sunday, and he taught English to our African students. He was a calm and easy-going guy who worried little, until the lights went out.

All of the houses had two bedrooms. Mike and his wife slept in one bedroom while their four-year-old daughter, Lisa, claimed the other. There was another member of the family, and her name was Wafita.

Wafita means "little black one" in Bemba, the local native language. Lisa loved the young black cat, who was less than a year old. Because Wafita was still a kitten, she would play any game at the drop of a hat. While Lisa slept in her single bed each night, Wafita always curled up next to her. There was no television in this African wilderness and only an occasional radio program. People made up their own entertainment, and Lisa and Wafita were an inseparable team.

Mike and his wife were already in bed when the lightning strike hit the transformer pole near the road. The huge flash told him the power had gone off throughout the area. "Oh, well," he said to his wife. "I'm glad it happened this late when we're already tucked in."

Stillness fell over the neighborhood, with the only sounds coming from the jungle behind their home. The constant singing of tree frogs, in concert with the cries of night birds, were the normal sounds that put them to sleep. However, tonight thunder booming through the valley would drown out much of that nocturnal music.

An hour passed while the couple slept. Suddenly, they heard Lisa shout, "Mommy, Daddy, come quick. There's a dragon in my room!"

"Go to sleep, Lisa," Mike yelled back. Then all was quiet once more.

A few minutes later, their sleep was interrupted again when their daughter cried out, "Mommy, Daddy, there's a monster in my room!"

"Mike, please see what's wrong with that girl. We'll never get any sleep if she keeps this up," Lisa's mom pleaded.

Mike got up and padded out of the bedroom. The tile floor felt cool under his bare feet as he started down the hall to his daughter's room. Thanks to the lightning, he could make out some things in the darkness.

He stopped at Lisa's door as yet another flash lit up the African sky and illuminated his daughter's room. In that brief instant he saw Lisa sitting up on her single cot that was placed against the wall. She sat straight and looked rigid, with her feet drawn up under her.

Mike was about to ask, "Lisa, what's going on?" but at that split second the room brightened and he saw something race across the floor followed by a loud *whap*. His mind raced. *What in the world was that?* he thought.

Lisa saw her father and exclaimed, "Daddy, look!" Mike peered into the shadows just as the thing dashed across the floor again, followed by the sound of *whap*!

Thunder rolled overhead as the sky brightened once more. This time Mike saw it. This time he saw the "monster/dragon" that Lisa had cried out about. The big cobra was coiled near her bed while its hooded head swayed five feet above the floor.

Mike stood frozen in the doorway. His jaw had dropped open in amazement, and he felt paralyzed with fright. *Whap!* The big snake struck at the small black cat again as she sped past it.

The cobra's sharp fangs had snapped just above Wafita's ear. When she reached the other side of the room, she stopped, turned, and crouched with her tail twitching with excitement. At the same time, the cobra pulled itself erect after missing with yet another strike.

Wafita shot off again, racing near the big snake, daring it to get her. What a wonderful game! The deadly reptile lashed down once more, this time barely missing the tip of the black tail.

Mike finally pulled himself out of the trance caused by the life-and-death drama he was watching. He sprang through the door and swept Lisa up in his arms. As he ran down the hall, he shouted to his wife, "Get out! Get out! There's a cobra in the house. Get out the front door. I've got Lisa!"

Mike leaped through the door, holding Lisa tightly in his arms. His wife followed seconds later. Next came Wafita at jet speed. As they ran toward their neighbor's yard, they turned and saw the big snake streaking through the grass toward them. Cobras can move swiftly when they're angry, and the family knew they had little time to waste.

Wafita was now leading the way. They were moving fast in the darkness, but they could still make out the snake's movements not far behind.

When they made it to their neighbor's yard, a bright light glared, but this time it was not lightning. Their neighbor stood holding a large flashlight, and its beam shone directly on the deadly snake as it closed in on them. In his other hand, the man held a twelve gauge shotgun that he raised and aimed. The cobra pulled itself up tall and then spread its hood, ready to strike.

A thunderous boom filled the night air and echoed down the African valley. The big snake flew into the air as it was struck by the fearful blast. Finally, it fell dead on the grass, its nighttime games over.

Soon a crowd of neighbors gathered. Lisa held Wafita in her arms and hugged her as Mike told everyone how the young kitten had saved his daughter's life. There in the dark African night, the little black one had played a deadly game of tag—and won.

DID YOU KNOW?

- Cobras can grow to be more than 14 feet in length.
- When alarmed, a cobra's neck will stretch and make itself into a broad hood.
- The reptile's venom contains powerful nerve toxins that are capable of killing people and large animals.

HALLOWEEN, SPIRITS, AND WITCH DOCTORS

Everyone was having a super time. Our Halloween party appeared to be a great success. The colored lanterns that Alicia and I had hung around the yard were dancing in the evening breeze.

Teachers from the college sat at decorated tables on the lawn, chatting and drinking punch while the little kids ran around chasing or playing games. Meanwhile, Joko and her older brother, Peter, sat with Alicia and me, taking everything in.

Earlier, Alicia had told a ghost story to our guests. It was about mummy-like monsters chasing teenagers through a graveyard while screaming at them and yelling out their names. "That was a wonderful story, Alicia. I think my knees are still trembling a bit from those dead monsters," Joko said.

"Thanks, Joko. Annie put me up to it. Since Americans are the only people who celebrate Halloween, we wanted everyone to hear about our spooky ghosts and goblins."

"Africans don't celebrate your Halloween, but we do have our own weird spirits, and they're around all the time, not just once a year," Peter chimed in. "And talk about scary!"

"You're kidding me. Like what?" Alicia quickly asked.

"Africans are very superstitious. Every village has a medicine man, or witch doctor as you guys call them, who uses fear and superstition in his practice. Most of them are really smart because they know everything about herbs, roots, and special leaves that they brew up for medicine. My dad says a lot of that stuff does help people with stomach problems or pain," Peter explained.

"If someone in the village was hurt badly, like bleeding from a serious wound or cut, would they take him to the medicine man?" I asked.

"Not if there is a clinic or a hospital nearby. Medicine men usually treat people with minor health problems. However, their main work is with villagers who think that black magic is causing some sort of illness or if they believe they are suffering from a curse or spell."

"That's truly amazing," Alicia interrupted. "If I wanted to put a curse on someone, say Annie, could I?"

"Maybe. Many Africans believe in curses. Let's say you have a serious argument with someone in the village. Then, a few days later you begin feeling dizzy. Perhaps that person paid the witch doctor to perform some black magic by placing a spell on you.

"Villagers also wear charms and fetishes to protect themselves from the spirits of the dead. Every house has at least one or two spirits watching over it. These are the souls of their relatives, ancestors who died long, long ago. People want these spirits to take care of them, so they praise them through tribal ceremonies that include chanting and dancing."

"Peter, Dad told you not to talk about this stuff. It's not healthy, and, besides, it scares me," Joko scolded her brother.

A small sliver of moon rose above the trees. Our little group hung onto every word Peter was saying, and he continued as though his sister had said nothing.

"You guys have to understand that all Africans believe in one supreme god; he's the god of the universe. Then there are several local gods who have control over their individual lives and their village."

"Like who?" I asked.

"Well, there is Vadam the water god. He controls the rivers and the lakes where people fish and collect drinking water. At the entrance to a village there is usually a large statue, maybe ten feet high, honoring Vadam. Around his wooden head he wears a headband of black feathers from various water birds. They droop down above his pitch-black eyes that have big white circles drawn around them. It's like he's always looking directly at you."

"He sounds evil," Alicia said with a shiver.

"Villagers believe idols like Vadam have souls, and they treat him like a god. When they arrive at their fishing holes, they chant and praise him. During dry spells women sing and dance for him, hoping he'll bring rain and clean water to drink."

"Peter, can't we talk about something else?" Joko asked.

"I'm almost done. I just wanted Annie and Alicia to know a little about village superstitions. The really bad god is Selema. She is the god of almost everything evil. When the sun goes down, many villagers lock themselves in their houses for the night. When it's black outside, sometimes an eerie high-pitched voice can be heard drifting in from the forest. It's Selema, floating into the village on the evening mist."

"Wow, talk about your ghost stories!" I exclaimed. "What does she do?"

"Villagers say Selema drifts invisibly among the straw and mud huts, sometimes disguising her voice as that of a small child. In the darkness, she begs for food or water and pleads to the family to let her in. The people fear her so much that they leave gourds of water and pieces of dried fish out on the doorstep.

"Should a child or unsuspecting visitor be foolish enough to open the door, Selema is capable of gaining possession of them by taking control of their minds and bodies. Once she has control, she can cause them to have serious accidents or even die by forcing them to throw themselves into the river."

I shuddered just as Peter's father walked up. "Hi, kids. Looks like you're having a very serious conversation"

"Not really," Peter answered. "Just talking about some of the teachers at school."

DID YOU KNOW?

- Tribal people who worship statues and wooden idols are called animistic.
- Religious practices play an important part in daily village life.
- A medicine man might throw ivory beads, shells, small bones, and other things and watch their patterns to help him read a person's future.
- Africans believe that an angry spirit can cause illness. A witch doctor can cure the illness using charms, salves, and potions made from roots and herbs.
- Villagers believe that a good witch doctor does things openly and an evil witch doctor operates in secret, preparing harmful potions and poisons.
- Rituals and ceremonies in African villages are often used to summon spirits to the real world so that their guidance can be sought.
- Warring tribes have been known to steal the gods and idols of other tribes. They feel that these stolen spoils of war can be added to their village and will make their tribe stronger.

LIONS DON'T EAT PEOPLE

We were walking home from school when one of the kids in our neighborhood told us that poachers had shot a female lion, but that her two cubs had survived. A family living down the road was caring for the little ones, he said.

When Dad got home, he agreed to walk Annie and me down to see the cubs. They were in a wire enclosure, sort of like a chicken coop. Both of the cubs were asleep in the warm sun.

Hearing us, they got up and sauntered over to check us out. We tried to pet them through the wire mesh, but it was difficult. "Dad, can we go in?" I asked.

"Be careful. They're just babies, but they still have sharp teeth and claws."

Annie rushed in first. She was only wearing a shirt and shorts, but she sat right down on the ground, and the delighted babies began climbing all over her. They purred as she petted them, and they tried to lick her face. "Come on in, Alicia! They're wonderful!"

I walked up to the threesome. I was dressed in long pants, not shorts. One of the cubs came up to me and rubbed against my leg. He was only about a foot tall, with short blondish yellow fur. He was so cute.

The little guy continued to rub against my pant leg while purring. Then, without warning, he turned and sank his teeth into my jeans at the knee. The bite hurt and I let out a yelp. The cub let go immediately and wandered back to Annie and his brother.

For weeks I wondered about the little lion and why he bit me. They had been so gentle with Annie. What was it about me? The bite had barely broken the skin on my knee. But are lions born mean? It wouldn't be long before I learned the answer to my question.

On a Saturday, Dad piled us all in the car, and we drove three hours through the forest on a narrow road. Big billowy clouds floated in the blue African sky. When the road ran along the river, we saw large fish eagles circling overhead as they prepared to dive and pluck fish from the warm water.

Soon the forest thinned and gave way to rolling grasslands. The African savanna is home to herds of antelope, wildebeest, zebra, and other large grazing animals and the big cats that prey upon them.

We finally arrived at an area that had been declared a national game reserve. No hunting was allowed in the fifty-mile-long park, but there was only one ranger to oversee all this vast wilderness.

Jim was the man in charge of the protected area. Sometimes Jim came to the college to present wildlife programs to the students. He and Dad had gotten along well, and he had invited our family to visit the reserve.

During our picnic lunch I asked our host, "Are lions born mean? Do they hunt people?" I explained my experience with the little cub to Jim.

Jim laughed, and then he explained that the cub had only tugged at my jeans because he was curious about the strange material. He assured me that if I had been wearing shorts like Annie, the accidental bite would never have happened.

"Come on, girls. I'll prove to you that lions are friendly animals." Jim asked Mom and Dad to stay and keep an eye on his camp, and we climbed into his open Jeep. We drove a mile or so before stopping on a little rise. From our vantage point, we could look down at a few trees growing on the open plain. Mounds of red earth, sometimes higher than two-story buildings, dotted the landscape like bladeless windmills. Some had large acacia trees growing on them.

"Those are ant hills," Jim said. "They're really termite mounds, but everyone calls them ant hills. Lion prides love to hang out on top of them. It gives them a great view of the savanna and a wonderful hunting advantage.

"Check out those shade trees." We looked down to where Jim was pointing. Annie and I gasped in unison, as if we were sharing a single breath. We were dumbstruck. Under the trees we saw lions. *Lots* of lions! There must have been twenty of the big beasts. "There's a pride for you. A family of moms, dads, babies, aunts, and uncles," Jim added.

"They rest in the shade during the heat of the day. Then they hunt in the late afternoon when it's cooler. They go after the big stuff like wildebeest and buffalo. They need a fair amount of food to feed such a large family. They're not the least bit interested in people, Alicia," the ranger added with a chuckle. "We're too small to provide much food for their family."

"There's no way that I'm going to prove it!" I exclaimed as I stared down from the open Jeep.

"Come on," the game ranger commanded while stepping from the vehicle. Annie jumped out, but Jim had to sort of gently pull me from the car.

"Where are we going?" I demanded. Jim pointed down the hill.

"NO WAY!" I shouted.

Scared to death but evidently having faith in our new friend, we slowly walked down the little hill. The lions looked up at us as we approached. When we reached the bottom, two big black-maned males rose and stood silently, watching our every move. We could see the muscles in their shoulders quiver in the sunlight. The thick black hair growing around their necks formed a heavy mane. They had such beautiful heads and such formidable jaws. It was like we were mesmerized. Indeed, they were the King of Beasts.

The pride was close now; not more than the length of a couple of tennis courts separated us. Jim whispered, "Turn left now, and we'll walk past the pride, and away from them." We moved quietly. I could almost feel their stares and smell their rangy wildness. Some of them were probably sizing us up for dinner.

We walked on, slowly. None of them moved; the two big males stood silently on guard. We circled back up the hill toward the Jeep. When we started climbing the little hill, one of the male guards sort of snorted and then lay down. Finally we were at the vehicle, and my sister and I scrambled in quickly. Jim, however, got in slowly, started the engine, and we drove off.

When we were out of sight of the pride, I exploded. "I have never been so scared in my entire life. Jim, I hope you don't do this often!"

"I drive by and say hello every couple of weeks, whenever the lion family is in the area. As I told you girls earlier, lions only hunt when they're hungry, and they only hunt big game so they can feed the entire family.

"When they attack, one will always leap on the broad

back of the animal. That's their favorite spot. It slows down the animal until other family members can help with the hunt. Without that big, broad back, lions wouldn't know what to do. When they saw us, they didn't see four legs and a broad back. No, they only saw stick figures walking across the clearing—silly little stick figures walking upright on our hind legs. What kind of game were we? Certainly nothing that interested that pride," Jim concluded.

"Dad, Mom, thank goodness we're stick figures!" I shouted as we drove into Jim's camp. Our parents had no idea what I was talking about, but we explained in great detail—all the way home.

DID YOU KNOW?

- The body of a male lion is more than six feet long, and he can have a three-foot-long tail.
- Male lions weigh up to 500 pounds. A female lion is slightly smaller.
- Lions will have litters of two to six cubs.
- Most lions are in Africa. However, a small number do live in India.
- Lions mainly live on savannas and grassy plains where large game is plentiful.
- Most of the hunting for the group is done by the females.

THOSE HAIRY CLOWNS AT VICTORIA FALLS

Suppose you were a contestant on a big TV quiz show and they asked you, 'What is the largest waterfall in the world?' What would you say?" I asked.

My older sister was lying on her bed enjoying a good book. Great way to pass the time on a hot African afternoon. "I don't know, Annie," she said, looking up from her novel. "I guess I'd try Niagara Falls for an answer."

"Buzzzzzzz! Incorrect answer," I chided. "For your information, dear sister, the absolutely biggest waterfall in the world is right here where we live. Victoria Falls is twice as wide as our Niagara Falls at home and twice as deep. Can you believe it?"

Alicia managed a feeble, "Gee, maybe someday we'll go see it," as she flipped over another page.

"Not someday. We're going this weekend," I replied.

"What? We've only been here a few months and we're going on another trip!" Alicia exclaimed. I reminded her that our dad was a real go-getter and that we had a lot of friends here who had never ventured out to see any of the wonders of Africa. Dad always said to grab these once-in-a-lifetime experiences when you have the chance.

It was a six-hour drive across the savanna to the Zimbabwe River. In the last hour we'd caught a glimpse of a large herd of zebra and a rare sighting of a mother cheetah with her two cubs. She and her young ones were resting on an ant hill, watching the activity of the zebra herd. "Alicia, are zebras white with black stripes, or black with white stripes?"

"Give it up, Annie. That's an old one," Alicia said with a sigh.

"Look up ahead," Dad shouted. In the distance we could make out a huge plume of white smoke billowing up thousands of feet in the air.

"Is that a fire?" Alicia asked. Dad said it wasn't a fire and it wasn't smoke. He told us the plume was water vapor rising above Victoria Falls.

"We're lucky it's summer," he continued. "During the rainy season there's so much water plunging down those gorges that you can't see a thing and it's tough to even get near the falls."

When we reached the river, we stopped at an old hotel a short distance from the falls. It was big and white and looked centuries old standing alone by the river. The nearest town was hours away.

Dad booked us a large room with four beds, each draped with mosquito netting. Protection from mosquitoes was absolutely necessary because of the risk of malaria. As we headed downstairs to check on lunch, I complained, "I'm starving. I could eat absolutely anything."

The large dining room had giant windows that swung open to the forest. Some tree limbs even poked through the open windows near our table. The sandwiches that we ordered had just arrived when ear-piercing screams broke out in high-pitched voices. More than twenty long-tailed monkeys appeared out of nowhere. The tree limbs swayed with their weight as they chattered above our table.

They had cute little faces with big black eyes and brown fur. "They always show up when the food arrives," our waiter said. "They're terrible beggars."

As we ate our sandwiches, they held out their little hands, pleading for food while making pitiful faces as though they were starving. Sometimes one would hang by its tail and hold out extended fingers to get our attention. Then, without warning, two little guys jumped down on the floor near us. For the next few minutes they did back flips and handstands and made funny faces to amuse us. We giggled and laughed at their antics, which made it very difficult to eat.

As we prepared to leave, we picked up fruit from a basket on our table. The little clowns were very gentle and polite when we handed them pieces of apples and bananas. Dad and Mom held some up to the monkeys on the tree limb, and they gratefully accepted the gifts. "They look like they're trying to say thank you," I offered. "They're so sweet!" As we walked out, the group of beggars munched joyously and then sprang quietly back into the forest.

We headed toward a small boat dock across the road from the hotel. An old African gentleman with gray hair gave us a friendly wave. He was sitting on the dock, holding a homemade fishing pole with its line dangling in the water. Beneath the little pier the Zambezi River rushed toward the giant falls.

As we chatted with him, he asked if we'd come to see the hippos. He informed us that a boat took visitors up the river every two hours. We were lucky because it would be here in just a few minutes. "No one should miss the big hippo herd," he added.

"How about it?" Dad asked. "You guys brave enough for a boat ride on the great Zambezi?" We all said yes, and the great adventure was on.

In a few minutes we could hear the sound of a small engine in the distance. As the craft came down the river, we could see that it was only about fourteen feet long and powered by a small outboard motor. Two African boatmen apparently served as its crew.

From the dock we looked out across the river, but it was so wide we couldn't see the other side. Just down the river we could hear the relentless thunder of Victoria Falls crashing nearly four hundred feet to the rocks at the bottom of the gorge.

The small boat pulled up to the dock. It was really only a dugout canoe with a motor. Alicia and I had the same thought as our eyes met. Do we really want to do this? What if the little motor conks out? That would leave us at the mercy of the crocodiles, the hippos, or possibly even a breathtaking ride over the falls. We were both having serious second thoughts when Dad said, "Come on, all aboard."

The boatmen pushed off, and we headed up the river, keeping near the shore to avoid the fast currents. As we put-putted upstream, we saw a few crocodiles floating silently near the shore. "Big river croc," one boatman said. Alicia and I looked at each other, rolling our eyes.

We rounded a bend in the river and the other man said, "Hippo dey!" Just ahead we could make out the snouts, eyes, and ears of the big beasts as they floated in the water. They were everywhere. Several hundred amphibious giants were enjoying the cool water under the hot African sun. Occasionally a big male would snort loudly and lift himself halfway out of the water in a show of strength and force.

We circled the herd quietly while taking a few pictures. Their eyes were glued on us, and their distrust was obvious. "Hippos bad!" the boatman said. He told us hippos killed more people in Africa than any other animal. They are very protective of their water holes, he explained. When fishermen intrude, the hippos sometimes get angry and tip their canoes and drown them. When game rangers kill bad hippos, they often find the beads of many fishermen in their stomachs, he added.

The herd started moving more, appearing agitated. Several males let out roars of warning that sounded very much like the roar of lions. "We go now," the boatman stated as he turned the little canoe and headed down river.

The thunder of the falls seemed almost deafening after the quiet waters of the hippo pool. As we climbed out on the dock, Dad asked, "Enjoy the ride, girls?" We had, but the hippo herd had been a little too close for comfort. Alicia put it best. "These sneakers are really happy to be back on dry land!"

DID YOU KNOW?

- Victoria Falls drops 355 feet into a gorge that is more than 5,500 feet wide.
- David Livingston was the first European to reach the falls in 1855.
- Livingston named the falls after the English queen, Queen Victoria.
- The hippopotamus can grow to 15 feet in length and to more than 5 feet tall. It can stay submerged for 10 minutes.
- Hippos go ashore at night to feed on grasses, but they sleep in or near the water.

AFRICANS ARE
COLOR BLIND

A big wedding was about to take place, and excitement filled the air at the college. Our good friend Joko and I were sprawled out on my bed while Annie sat at the small white desk in my bedroom.

We had heard thunder rolling around the valley earlier, and we wondered if bad weather would hamper the wedding tomorrow. Our little slumber party should have ended by now, but we were too excited to sleep. Instead, we'd been yakking about the bride and groom and what we would be wearing to the social event of the year, rain or no rain.

The three of us knew Tunde because he was a teacher at the college. Tunde was a neat guy in his mid-twenties who was liked by everyone. But no one, absolutely no one, knew the bride. Her name was Shanta, and she was supposed to be young and beautiful. However, there were rumors, quiet chitchat behind the scenes, because this African beauty was not a local girl but from a faraway tribe.

Joko is a really smart girl, even for a ten-year-old. "My dad and mom have been talking about the wedding," she said. "They really like Tunde because he's a friend to everyone and he is also from our tribe."

"Tunde's a Bemba, from the local tribe?" I asked.

"Well, of course," Joko shot back. "What did you think he was?"

"Gosh, Joko. Sorry," I answered. "Annie and I are from faraway places. How are we supposed to know who's from what tribe?"

Annie joined the lively discussion. "What's all this got to do with the wedding? Are people like your parents worried about Shanta because she's from a different tribe?"

Joko sat up on the bed and crossed her legs like she was preparing to do battle. "I've heard," she stated, "that when a white marries a black in the United States, that is often called a mixed marriage. True?"

"People of all races and backgrounds get married in California, Joko. They just get married like everybody else," I stated. "I've never heard of the term 'mixed' used like that before."

"I may be wrong, but I think I read it in a story where a white guy married a black woman," she insisted. "Anyway, it doesn't matter. My dad said the wedding tomorrow will be a mixed marriage because Tunde is Bemba, and Shanta comes from the Meru tribe up north. When I asked him about his comment, he said it didn't matter what skin color people have, but marrying outside one's tribe is another matter."

"You're right," Annie joined in. "I've never heard anyone here ever mention skin color. Like the other day at school when my teacher called me in from the playground. I heard him tell a kid, 'Go get that girl in the blue dress; her mother is here.' He didn't say, 'Go get that white girl; her mom is here to pick her up.' "

I picked up where Annie left off. "Dad claims that Africans are color blind. He said there were teachers at the college from Canada, North America, South America, Europe, and the Orient. He is convinced that the African headmaster and other African teachers are totally unaware of any skin differences. He is positive that there is no color prejudice among African people."

"Your dad is right," Joko said. "We don't see skin color, but I guess we get a little uptight about other tribes. You see, our tribe is like a large family, even though there may be thousands of us. There can be several hundred villages spread for miles, but the people still belong to the same tribe.

"My father talks about our politics and our customs. As children we're raised following these Bemba customs, and from our elders we learn about our tribal history, rituals, and traditions.

"Shanta was raised the same way, only she comes from the Meru tribe, not the Bemba. Sometimes we are suspicious of other tribes and their ways. These fears can make us slow to accept their people."

The next day the college chapel was lovely, filled with fresh flowers and smiling guests. Tunde looked handsome in his black suit and silk tie. He appeared to be a little nervous as he waited by the altar with the best man and the minister.

Joko, Annie, and I were sitting together near the front so we wouldn't miss a thing. When the music began at the rear of the chapel, we looked back to see Shanta walking down the aisle in a beautiful multi-colored silk dress with an elegant head scarf. She was drop-dead gorgeous in a swirl of blues, oranges, and reds. No one cared if she was Meru, Bemba, American, or from Mars. They were a lovely couple who would bring more joy to this already happy campus.

DID YOU KNOW?

- The Bemba tribe is one of the Bantu-speaking groups. There are hundreds of Bantu languages, with more than 200 million people in Africa speaking some form of Bantu.
- A tribe is a group of people who share a common ideology, language, and traditions.
- Tribes usually work together on agricultural projects, domestic chores, trade, and warfare. They often perform ceremonial functions as a group.
- Tribe members can live in small villages or in larger collections of villages.
- To be easily identified, some members wear tribal paint markings or tribal scars.

The Haunted Yacht

My sister and I were sorry that we didn't get to complete our tour through the lake country. Our experience with the baby elephant and her mother was unbelievable, but it certainly brought that trip to an abrupt stop.

But maybe Lady Luck was on our side after all. We knew that something was up when we saw a new Land Rover pull into our driveway. An African man was driving, and Dad sat next to him. The two chatted happily as they walked toward the house.

Annie and I met them at the front door, where we were introduced to Fred. "Fred is the official driver for the college," Dad said. "They want us to go up to lake country again and check on those two village schools. Fred's going to drive this time. Want to give it another try? We're leaving next week."

We were both thrilled at the thought of another adventure and were raring to go. "Did you tell Fred about the elephants on our last trip?" I asked.

"Yes, he's heard all about that wild day. It's going to be better this time. Fred knows those roads well," Father added.

"I grew up in a village not far from the great lake," Fred

offered. "I speak the local native languages, and I was also schooled in French."

Our trip to the lake country would take us near the Zaire border. In the old days the country was called the Congo, and most of its African residents speak some French. About half of the people live in villages on the French Congo side of the border, and the rest reside on the British side.

Life with border tribes is interesting because they pay little or no attention to which country claims their land. The villagers consider it to be their land, and they cross the border daily and swear loyalty only to their own tribe.

The day finally came, and we were on our way to the lake country. Fred was an excellent driver. He made good time, yet he was very careful about keeping a watchful eye out for villagers or wild animals along the way. We kept looking for elephants as we passed through the canyons and hills where we had met Baby Elephant. Soon those hills were behind us, and we hadn't seen any of that herd.

Finally we reached the shores of Lake Mweru, the largest lake in the lake country. We stopped near an old two-story house where we were supposed to spend the night. The district commissioner, or head government official, lived here with his wife. Apparently, they hadn't received our telegram because no one was home.

It was late afternoon, and we looked at one another, wondering what we were going to do. Dad felt it would be too crowded for the four of us to sleep in the car. "I guess we have to rough it and bed down on the ground. Let's hope the mosquitoes don't fly away with us," he said.

Annie pointed out at the lake and said, "What's that?" We could see something floating in the water several hundred yards offshore.

"It's an old boat," Fred answered. "An old, broken down yacht. It was once used to patrol the lake, but it hasn't run for years. It just sits there rotting and rusting away."

"But it's big," Annie continued. "If we had some way to get out there, I'll bet it has bunks and places to sleep."

"You're probably right," Dad chimed in. "It could protect us from the sand fleas and mosquitoes that are thick here on the beach." Hearing that, we split up and began searching the area in hopes of finding some sort of small boat.

In a few minutes Fred called to us. "Over here. This will work!" We all hotfooted it over to him and found him looking down at a native dugout canoe. "It's in good shape. It'll get us out there and back," he added.

The two men paddled the log that some local villagers had burned and hollowed out to make a canoe. The lake was calm under the sinking sun. Occasionally a fish would break the water's surface near the little boat. Annie and I kept a sharp eye out for crocodiles. Eek! The very thought of them made me shiver with fear.

In a few minutes we reached the old patrol boat and tied up at the stern, or rear end as we call it in California. We climbed the rusted ladder up to the deck and surveyed the old wreck. Down below we found four cabins with double-decker bunk beds in each one. There was a small galley, or kitchen, if you prefer, so we were all set for the night.

"All we need now is the nice dinner that the district commissioner was supposed to have ready for us," I complained. I had just gotten the words out of my mouth when Dad said he had found some fishing line and hooks.

"Girls, there's a couple of pieces of bread left in the backpack. Put some water on it and make it into a dough for fish bait," Dad instructed. "Maybe we'll get some luck and have dinner after all," he said.

And luck we had. Annie put a small piece of dough on a hook and threw the line overboard, holding the ball of fish line in her other hand. Minutes later I did the same.

"Dad!" Annie screamed. "I've got one. Help me!" Dad rushed to her side as her fish line cut swiftly through the darkening lake water. Together they pulled up the line hand-over-hand until a big fish landed on the deck. It flopped wildly as Annie tried to hold it down with her sneaker.

"Man, look at the size of that thing!" Dad exclaimed. The big bass was more than two feet long, and it must have weighed at least four pounds. "Nice going, Annie. There's our dinner," he said proudly.

"Hey, you guys, over here. I've got one, too!" I yelled. We wrestled the second bass up on the deck. It was almost as large as Annie's.

"Alicia, it's a whale," Dad shouted. "We're going to have some kind of fish dinner tonight." The sun had slipped below the tall palm trees lining the shore, and the night noises of Africa were starting to sing. First the tree frogs started with their harmonizing voices. Then they were joined by the crickets with their shrill soprano chorus. Occasionally a large bullfrog would toss in his two cents' worth with a booming bass croak.

The four of us gathered in the little kitchen below deck. Annie and I watched as Fred and Dad tried to light the propane gas stove. In no time they had the old thing humming with a nice blue flame. "Girls, please go up on deck and get the fish so Fred and I can clean them," Dad said.

It was starting to get dark. We ran down the dim passageway, and our footsteps made quite a noise on the old wooden floor. When we reached the stern of the boat where we'd caught the big bass, Annie asked, "Where are they?" "Isn't this where we left them?"

"They're here, Annie. It's really dark and we just have to look a little," I answered. Feeling with my hands, I found the fish, or what used to be the fish. As I ran my fingertips over the bare bones, I let out a shrill scream. Fred and Dad were at my side in seconds.

"What is it, Alicia?" Dad asked urgently. "Are you all right?"

"The fish! Look at the fish!" I managed. They knelt as Fred produced a flashlight from his pocket. In the circle of light the four of us stared down open-mouthed at our supposed to be dinner. Except now, only the skeletons of two large African lake bass lay on the deck. There was not a shred of meat anywhere, just cleaned and polished fish bones. Even the big round eyes of the bass were missing.

"Holy smoke!" Dad said in a half whisper, like maybe there was someone or something lurking nearby that could hear him. "Fred, have you ever seen anything like this before?"

Fred told us that fish eagles can clean fish quickly, but they're only out in the daylight hours and not at night. Also, he said, fish eagles don't clean the skeletons so thoroughly.

The last rays of daylight were hanging on as the four of us stood there on the old boat and looked at one another. Fred was the first to speak. He asked Dad if it was okay for him to take the dugout canoe and row back to shore. It wasn't the fish bones that worried him, he said, but he would like to sleep on shore because he couldn't swim. "I was going to bring it up earlier, but if you don't mind?"

Hearing approval, our African friend climbed down the rusted ladder to the canoe and began paddling toward the shore. When he reached the spot where our vehicle was he yelled to us to wish us a good night.

"Well, girls, we still have some graham crackers in the backpack. Let's go have dinner," Dad said cheerfully.

After crackers and water, we settled in the cleanest cabin. We had discovered a couple of old army blankets earlier and had decided that we would all sleep in the same cabin—just in case. Annie and I would share the upper bunk while Dad took the lower.

It was now pitch-black outside the little round porthole window, and the night noises were growing louder. A big white moon had pushed itself above the palms, and the three of us had dozed off when a loud crashing sound made us sit upright with a start. The old yacht rocked back and forth and then settled quietly. Dad had just turned on the flashlight when the big *boom* sound came again and the boat shook under the attack.

"It feels like something is ramming the boat," Dad said, trying to keep his voice calm. He shined the flashlight out the porthole, illuminating the dark waters of the lake. There, ringing our rotting old boat, was a huge herd of hippos. Their eyes, ears, and snouts showed clearly in the moonlight. We could see them so well that Dad turned off the flashlight. At that moment a big bull lifted himself up, and the water turned white as he churned his legs lunging forward toward the boat. The boom noise sounded again as he rammed into the aging hull.

"Dad, what's happening?" Annie asked with the same fear in her voice that I felt inside. "Are they trying to sink the yacht?"

We held onto the bunks to keep our balance as yet another assault made our temporary home rock in the water. "Remember the hippos at Victoria Falls?" Dad asked. "The boatman told us hippos protect their own watering holes. This old patrol boat is painted white and it stands out clearly in the moonlight. They probably think it's an enemy of some sort and they're trying to sink it. They may do this every time there's a full moon."

We sat silently looking out the porthole, waiting for the next bull to attack. They took turns battering our fragile shelter until they finally swam away.

"Gee, that was fun," Annie cracked. "I wonder what the next act will bring."

"Don't even say that, Annie. We're lucky that this old tub held together. It's a long swim to shore, and we know there are crocodiles out there."

As we looked out, the moon was now overhead, lighting up the once dark water. Indeed, every few minutes we did see a lake croc float silently by. We knew for sure that a long swim to the shore was not an option.

By this time it was two o'clock in the morning, and I couldn't keep my eyes open any longer. Annie had dozed off some time ago, while Dad now lay quietly on the lower bunk. It felt so good to finally rest. It had been a long day and a very exciting evening with the hippo attack and the circling crocodiles. *My goodness*, I thought, *what else could possibly happen?*

The old yacht floated quietly on the lake while the three of us slept. It must have been near daybreak when Dad nudged me gently. "Wake up, Alicia. I hear noises. Something's on the boat."

I sat up quickly and slid off the bunk onto the floor. The hair on the back of my neck stood out. In the distance I could hear a scratching sound like when kids run their fingernails along a chalkboard. As I listened, it grew louder, like hundreds of nails scratching and clawing their way down the passageway toward our cabin.

"Annie, wake up!" Dad shouted. The three of us listened as the scratching sounds grew louder. Dad told us to stand back as he swung open the cabin door and flashed his light down the hallway. "I don't believe this!"

he exclaimed as he slammed the door shut. "Girls, hand me those blankets!"

As we followed his instructions, he told us that an army of cockroaches was coming down the passageway. He said they were huge, each one about five inches in length. We knew that cockroaches at home were tiny, not even an inch long. But the sound of these monster roaches scrambling down the wooden hallway made Annie and me almost freeze with terror.

He was now on his knees stuffing the end of the heavy wool army blanket into the space under the door. Annie and I were scared speechless, but somehow I managed to utter, "I guess we know what happened to our fish dinner." My sister gasped as she realized the seriousness of our situation.

"We'll be all right, girls," Dad reassured us. "They can't get in here if we keep the space under the door stuffed with these heavy blankets."

The loud scratching noise nearly stopped as the army of ugly roaches reached our cabin door. However, within seconds, the scratching sound was replaced by a munching kind of noise. "For heaven's sake! They're eating the blanket!" Dad spurted out. And munch they did.

For nearly an hour the little beasts chewed and ate the heavy wool material almost as fast as Dad could shove it under the door. They really wanted to get to us!

They had devoured most of one blanket, and we were getting ready to stuff in the other one when the munching ceased. Then, with their bellies apparently full, the army marched off down the passageway and down to their home at the bottom of the boat.

The three of us sat on the floor, sort of collapsed, as the scratching sound faded in the distance. Through the little porthole we could tell that the sun had come up. "The sunrise may have saved us," Dad offered. "It's well known that cockroaches always stop whatever they're doing and head for home at the first sign of the sun."

"Sort of like vampires," Annie joked. We all laughed as we got up and made our way to the deck. In the distance Fred waved and we waved back. It had, indeed, been quite a night on the old haunted yacht. We were not sunk by the hippos or taken by the lake crocodiles. Even the determined cockroach army had failed.

Like he is prone to do sometimes, Dad cracked a joke. "Hey, why don't we spend another night here?" Having said that, he ran and jumped into the canoe next to Fred before Annie and I could throw him overboard.

DID YOU KNOW?

- Cockroaches have flat, oval bodies and long, threadlike antennae.
- Cockroaches eat both plant and animal material.
- They like to live in warm, dark places.
- They are nocturnal, so they mainly come out at night.
- They are among the oldest living creatures on earth—320 million years old.
- One female cockroach can give birth to 35,000 offspring in one year.

Is Santa a Witch Doctor?

Our little brick house was just across the road from the college where I taught. All of the students were African, including a number of young married men who lived in small houses with their wives and children.

Many of these families had only lived in remote areas far from any towns or cities. Like most, their villages had a medicine man or witch doctor, as foreigners liked to call them. As a result, they grew up with tales of evil spirits and magical things, which caused many of them to be quite superstitious.

It was early December when I asked several teacher friends if Santa Claus had ever paid a visit to the children living on campus. The reply was no, but the college principal said he had no objection if I would like to be the first to play Santa. He reminded me, however, that Santa Claus is more American and that many countries refer to the merry old gentleman as Father Christmas.

It sounded like fun, so a date was set for a big Christmas party for the kids. Hundreds of African children and their mothers would attend. The great hall would be filled with babies, toddlers, and school-aged youngsters, and I was anticipating that a wonderful time would be had by all.

There was a small town a few miles from the college, and the local merchants were most generous with donations of small gifts and candy for the occasion.

My next effort was to put together a proper costume. Father Christmas is known to wear a long red robe. So, with a little help from friends, cloth was cut and a handsome robe was fashioned and sewn, along with a red cap adorned by a white furry ball on the end. A white cotton beard and mustache finished off the jolly outfit.

Soon the fateful afternoon arrived. From our house across the dirt road from the school, I could see streams of children heading toward the great hall. Most were accompanied by their mothers, who often held one child by the hand and had another baby tied securely to their backs.

The great hall was a large auditorium built of brick. It had huge Danish-style wooden windows throughout. They were always swung open in order to provide maximum cooling during the warm African days. It was here that all assemblies were held, including Sunday religious services.

The big moment finally arrived, and I crossed the road to the campus and headed toward the great hall. Several of my African and British buddies waited outside the main entrance with large cartons of toys and candy.

As Father Christmas, I carried a large red sack that contained some candy, but it was mainly stuffed with paper so it would retain its round shape. The real goodies would be distributed by my friends after Father Christmas made his grand entrance. I was so fat with the pillows hidden under my robe that I could scarcely walk.

As I prepared to enter the hall, I noticed a bicycle leaning against the building. Why not? Everybody rode bicycles here. They were the main source of local transportation, so why wouldn't Father Christmas arrive on one? What a great idea! Last minute, but a real touch of genius, I thought.

My friends threw open the big double doors, and Father Christmas rode into the great hall aboard his bike. Everyone stared as I shouted, "Ho-Ho-Ho" in a voice that boomed and echoed up to the high ceilings.

Unfortunately, the next few moments are difficult to describe. Five or six hundred pairs of wide eyes were frozen on the bicycle rolling down the aisle toward them and the big red figure that sat on top.

The expected "Hooray for Santa," or rather, "Hooray for Father Christmas," never came. Instead, as if in one voice, the packed hall was filled with a huge blood-curdling scream.

Then suddenly, one frightened youngster darted out in the aisle in the path of my speeding bike. Swerving to miss the child, my bike crashed, and Father Christmas and his bag of goodies sailed gracefully over the handlebars and several rows of seats.

The deafening noise of screams and cries continued as African mothers and their children fled in panic out every possible exit. Some mothers, not fortunate enough to be near a door, actually threw their toddlers out the large Danish windows onto the lawn and then jumped out after them. According to my fellow teachers, it was absolute bedlam.

A stunned Father Christmas slowly pulled himself out from behind a row of seats and peered out at the now empty great hall. At that moment, a three-year-old boy dashed past in a desperate attempt to escape. Somehow I managed to grab the child while freeing myself from the long red robe that was wrapped around my neck. The boy screamed deathly screams, but I held him gently and sat down in the middle of the aisle with him on my lap.

Producing a now rather crushed Hershey candy bar from my sack of goodies, I removed the paper and began eating it while offering the youngster the other half.

Bingo! Every kid in the world recognizes a Hershey bar when he sees one! As the two of us sat on the floor of the now empty hall eating candy, small black heads could be seen peeking over the edge of the windows. My newfound friend continued smacking his lips while waving a Snickers bar at his friends.

Slowly, a few kids crept back into the hall. First they entered in silent distrust, then by the dozens with loud and joyous approval as gifts and candy were passed out by Father Christmas and his helpers. Soon the great hall was filled once again.

Later, when it was all over, I realized that the African children and their mothers must have thought that the big red figure on the speeding bike was indeed an evil spirit. After all, most of these families came from remote villages where the likes of Santa Claus or Father Christmas were unknown.

So, after a very shaky start, it turned out to be a wonderful Christmas party with gifts, music, and singing. It ended as darkness settled over the school and the jungle that surrounded it.

And, it was about this time that pedestrians on the little dirt road reported to police that they had witnessed an eerie sight. They had watched a large, fat figure limp across the road toward the staff houses. Whatever it was, they said, it appeared to be cloaked in red and it was dragging a twisted looking bicycle behind it.

DID YOU KNOW?

- The roots of witchcraft run deep in Africa, even though missionaries tell of the millions of Africans who have abandoned tribal lore and embraced Christianity.
- Catholic missionaries have been among the most successful in persuading tribes to trade their juju dolls and fetishes for the rosary beads and crucifixes of the church.
- Some well-educated Africans still choose to return to their village medicine men when faced with serious illness.
- Black magic is the use of magical power with evil intent.
- White magic is used for good purposes.
- Village medicine men have considerable skill in the use of herbal medicine and traditional remedies.
- In 1976, the World Health Organization recommended including tribal healers in the health teams working in African countries.

TELLING TALES IN THE TREETOPS

It was a blustery Saturday morning with cloudy African skies dumping rain one hour and then clearing the next. Our parents were driving to the little town of Kitwe to do some shopping. We asked if we could visit Joko and Peter instead of going with them.

Mrs. Lonwani was in the kitchen when we arrived, and she told us the kids were out back in the tree house. They had a big baobab tree in the yard where Peter and Joko had worked hard to build a little hideaway. "Come on up," Peter yelled down from his high perch. It hadn't rained for a while, so the board ladder nailed up the side of the tree was dry.

"Annie, Alicia, mwapoleni," Joko greeted us in the local language when we reached the platform. "I didn't know you guys were coming over. What a nice surprise."

Joko was always such a sweet person, happy and fun to be around. Even though Peter was older and a boy, he was a good guy and very considerate, I thought. They had done a wonderful job on their little house in the sky. It was really quite large, big enough to sleep four kids, and it had a water-proof roof made of palm fronds.

As they offered us pillow seats on the floor, we compli-
mented them on their roost so high off the ground. "You
guys have done a super job building this. People could live
up here," Annie offered.

"It's high and dry, even when it's raining," Peter replied.
"Safe from animals on the ground. All we have to do is keep
an eye out for tree snakes."

"Yuck. You could have gone all day without bringing
that up," I sighed.

The sky grew dark and suddenly it began raining again.
The forest behind us smelled so fresh and the sound of the
water rushing off the palm fronds was soothing. "Sometimes
we tell stories when we're up here," Joko said. "Africans like
to tell stories about their people. Funny little ones we call
folk tales."

"We have folk tales, too," I exclaimed. And, with a little
encouragement, I told the story about Paul Bunyan and his
giant blue ox, Babe. It was fun being so high up in the giant
tree and telling tall tales. It was turning into a fun afternoon.

"Here's one for you," Peter said. "It's called 'The Chief
and the Crocodile.' Every African boy loves this story.

"Once there was a beautiful stream that flowed by a large
village. The stream separated the village from the outside
world, so visitors had to wade across to visit their friends and
relatives. If a villager wanted to leave, he would also have to
ford the wide waterway before he began his journey.

"Even though the stream was beautiful, the people hated
it because it was home to a huge, ugly crocodile. Every year
the big creature caught and carried away several villagers,
including some of the chief's own wives. This sad situation
went on for several years. It had gotten so bad that no one
came to visit anymore, and the local residents were afraid to
risk their lives to travel outside the village.

"Finally, one day the chief called a tribal council with the entire village attending. 'The evil monster that lives in our clear stream has caused our lives to be unbearable. He has taken so many of our friends and family that we must put an end to him. In every way he has made our village into a prison. I will give one hundred pounds of gold to the person who can bring an end to his tyrannical reign.'

"Menkon was the strongest warrior in the tribe. He could throw a spear farther and straighter than anyone, and every inch of him was tough and brave. 'I'll take care of the man-eater,' he stated, as he headed toward the wide stream carrying ropes and weapons.

"For ten days and ten nights the mighty warrior stalked the giant croc along the stream banks, laying traps and lures for it. Finally, upset and frustrated with his failure, he took his spear and panga knife and stood in the middle of the stream to force a showdown with the beast.

"The next day, children walking along the stream found several weapons, including a large spear and panga knife. The knife was broken and the spear was so severely bent that it was useless. The youngsters took these broken weapons back to the chief. 'Alas, poor Menkon is dead,' the chief grieved.

"A witch doctor from another village came, with all of his medicines and juju charms. 'I will free you all from this water-devil that controls your lives,' he told the chief. Having said that, he camped by the stream and poured many potions and poisons into the water. Nothing worked, so the next day he poisoned a large fresh fish and held it over the water. The stream seemed to explode as the croc lunged out, grabbing the fish and the witch doctor all in one bite. Then all disappeared beneath the surface.

"The people of the village were deeply saddened. It was clear that they would have to live the rest of their lives in isolation, far from their friends and families, because of this most evil of monsters.

" 'Don't give up yet,' Ocon shouted.

" 'Who are you?' the noble chief demanded. 'You're a mere boy, a teenager. You are no match for this water creature!' The young Ocon was not a strong warrior, but he was very bright and had good ideas. Reluctantly the chief gave his permission for Ocon to plan his attack on the killer crocodile.

"First he put a large fish on a stick and allowed it to float down the stream. Within seconds the mammoth croc crushed it in his jaws and swallowed it. The next day Ocon floated a large piece of wild pig down the stream, and watched as the same thing happened. Gulp, the pig was gone.

"That night, Ocon told his parents to expect to be rich the next day because he would kill the beast that ruled the stream. They were worried when he set off with a large papier-mache doll that he had made. The doll was the exact image of himself, clothes and all. He even put a dirty shirt on the doll so that it would smell human. Last, he filled the doll with cement powder so it would keep its shape. Then, he floated his doll-double down the stream.

"Pow! The great crocodile came straight up from the bottom of the creek and snatched the doll in his powerful jaws. Without stopping, he dove to the bottom to enjoy his meal of the Ocon boy from the village. However, as he ate, he could feel a very large stomachache coming on.

"The next morning, with the help of ten men, Ocon put ropes around the dead croc and they pulled it from the bottom of the stream. The monster was heavy now and solid as a rock. As the crocodile had chomped its last victim, water had mixed with the dry cement powder and soon the mixture turned into concrete. The evil one was dead; he had turned to stone.

"People cheered and praised Ocon for his clever victory.

The village was saved and the chief rewarded the youngster with one hundred pounds of gold.

"That was many years ago, but the giant crocodile still stands there by the stream. It is a statue that represents evil and the knowledge that good will always prevail."

"A super story, Peter. I loved it," I said.

"I've got one. It's a story I first heard when I was five. It's called 'How the Hyena Got His Laugh,' " Joko told us.

"One day in the middle of the jungle, all of the animals were looking for something to eat. It was beginning to get dark, so one little hyena went searching for frogs and mice—anything to feed his hunger. After hours of hunting, he had found nothing.

"The next morning he was starving when he heard the chirping of birds. *I think I'll have a bird for breakfast*, he thought. When he caught a bird, he was so hungry that he ate it in one gulp, feathers and all. However, in a few minutes he felt something caught in his throat. He tried to cough it up but couldn't.

"It was a feather from the bird, lodged firmly in his throat. After a while, the feather began to tickle and tickle. The hyena tried to remain quiet, but he couldn't. So, he began to laugh and laugh. And, try as he may, whenever he opened his mouth, out came this weird crazy laugh. That happened a long time ago, but that's how the hyena got his laugh."

"That's a cute story," Annie said, smiling.

"I've got another one," Peter jumped in. "It's called 'Why Monkeys Live in Trees.'

"One night two lions slipped into a village and stole a large fish drying on a pan. When they got back to their home in the jungle one of them said, 'Here, I'll divide it.' But the other one did not trust his friend so he insisted that someone else cut it fairly.

"Just then, a monkey came along and they asked him to divide the fish equally, and the monkey readily agreed. However, when he broke the fish in two pieces, he made one piece larger than the other. 'Oh, my goodness, they are not equal halves,' he said. So he began eating from the bigger portion.

" 'What are you doing?' one of the lions growled.

" 'I'm going to eat part of this bigger piece to make it even with the other,' the monkey replied. But, as he chomped away on the tasty fish, that piece soon became smaller than the other. So, switching them back again, he began munching on the other portion.

"Soon, the lions realized what the scoundrel monkey was up to, so one said, 'Give us the fish and we will divide it up ourselves.'

" 'No, you don't want to do that,' the hairy tree climber argued. 'You might get angry and begin to fight. Here, this won't take much longer.' And so he switched from one piece to the other until the entire fish was inside his fat little belly.

"Seeing that they had been tricked, the two lions let out mighty roars that made the monkey's hair stand on end. He bolted for the nearest tree and shot up it with the lions in hot pursuit.

" 'You've tricked us this time, Mr. Monkey, but you are the loser,' the king of the jungle roared. 'Did you enjoy your stolen meal? We hope so because this is the last time that you will ever set foot down here with the rest of the family of animals.'

"And, from that time on, the monkey and his kinfolk were forbidden to roam the jungle floor. They now must live high in the trees, alone without friends and neighbors."

The sun popped out from behind the clouds just as Mom and Dad called up to us to let us know they were home. Annie and I climbed down from the tree house and thought what a fun afternoon it had been telling stories so high in the treetops.

DID YOU KNOW?

- Most cultures save and pass on their traditions by telling folk tales. In addition to folk tales, African tribes also use song and dance to transfer their beliefs and rituals to the younger generation.
- Many European countries used fairy tales to transmit cultural information to their children.
- The terms *folk tale, folk music,* and *folk dance* meant something that had been created by the people, rather than something that was originated by a king or ruler of a country.

THE DEADLY PICNIC

It was a bright Saturday morning when Peter said, "Hey, Joko, want to go on a picnic?" His sister was quick to say yes.

Mrs. Lonwani was busy in the kitchen when they approached her. "Mom, could we make a lunch and go down to the river for a picnic?" Joko asked.

Her mother was thoughtful for a moment. Then she answered, "Well, I guess so, if you promise to be careful." The two kids promised as Peter dashed to the pantry to fetch the picnic basket.

Minutes later they ran across the back lawn, then out the gate and into the forest that Africans called "the bush." Almost immediately tall trees began to block out much of the sun, and Joko had to run hard to keep up with her athletic brother. The youngsters heard many sounds as they made their way through this place that served as home for a variety of wild animals.

Peter led and Joko followed, carefully keeping to the path. As they walked, they scuffed their feet on the ground, causing dirt and small pebbles to fly forward on the trail. The kids had been trained to make this kind of ruckus while walking in the bush so that sleeping snakes would wake and flee. Often, it was only on a path that the sun was able to shine through the heavy foliage. It was here, on this warmth, that deadly reptiles loved to nap.

After twenty minutes they broke out of the bush and spotted the palm trees and boulders that meant they had reached the river. When the brother and sister found a grassy patch, they stopped and spread out their picnic blanket. The spot they chose was high above the water, providing them with an excellent view of the area. Here the river was wide, about the width of a football field.

When they finished lunch, Peter stood and said, "I'm going to wash these plastic plates, Joko. If I don't, we'll have a bunch of ants with us when we get home." Then he walked down the bank to the river's edge, rolled up his trousers, and waded into a foot of water. When small, lapping waves began to touch his bare legs, he stopped, bent over, and dipped the plates into the water.

The river felt cool on his bare feet after the hot, red clay earth along the bank. High above, the warm afternoon sun caused perspiration to form on his forehead. *How peaceful it is here*, he thought, as he waved to Joko.

With skilled fingers he gave the little plates one final rinse. Then he straightened up and shook them briskly in the hot, tropical breeze. As he prepared to return to the riverbank just a few feet away, it happened.

Peter cried out in terror as he was violently ripped from his footing. His mouth was open, still filled with the scream, and his eyes were wide with fright as his arms flailed the humid African air. As if in slow motion, he clawed the sky for handholds as he crashed in the murky water with a great splash.

Joko jumped to her feet in horror, shrieking as she watched her thrashing brother fight for his life. With his free foot, Peter kicked desperately and repeatedly at his unseen assailant.

From her higher place on the riverbank, Joko could see what he could not. The huge male crocodile, more than fourteen feet in length, continued to wave his long tail in sweeping movements in the water while his strong legs back paddled. Slowly he towed Peter away from the shore toward the center of the river, much like a boat backing away from a dock.

The young African's water-choked shouts continued as he pounded the surface with his arms and kicked violently at the place where his ankle was locked in solid jaws.

In deeper water his cries for help stopped abruptly as the huge beast suddenly submerged. Peter's hands grasped hopelessly at the surface and then they too disappeared.

Then, all was still. Only ripples gliding out to deeper water and those that lapped against the riverbank paid witness to the tragedy that had just occurred.

Peter's hysterical sister turned and ran, wailing through the bush in search of help. At the bottom of the river the creature stared at his prey through small, beady eyes, looking for signs of life. Seeing none, the carnivorous croc swam to the other side where the bank was steeper and entered his underwater lair.

Many years ago, he had dug this large hole in the side of the embankment, and now it served as a secret den. The entrance was hidden well below the river's surface, and it was here that he stored his kills until they were properly aged and suitable to eat.

Pushing with his snout and strong front legs, the river monster coaxed the still body into his hidden subterranean meat locker. Satisfied, the croc reversed out of the lair and swam a few yards down the river to bask in the hot African sun.

Later that afternoon, two African game rangers appeared at the water's edge. They were followed by a large group of wide-eyed villagers and Peter's crying sister. Spotting the big crocodile sleeping on a sandbank across the river, the rangers adjusted their rifle scopes, and powerful shots rang out, echoing down the winding river and out into the bush. The crocodile pushed off from his warm sunning beach one last time before sliding back into the dark water.

The villagers stared, and the marksmen reloaded as the huge man-eater floated lifelike momentarily before rolling over, his belly up in the sure death sign of the species. The old warrior had undoubtedly been king of this part of the river. Now the king was dead, but alas, it was too late for poor Peter Lonwani.

Later the sun set over the gruesome scene on the river, and the palm and acacia trees cast weird shadows across the darkening water. The crocodile had long since been skinned by the villagers.

As darkness began to settle over the jungle, the night birds in the trees above the dead crocodile's lair suddenly fell silent as sounds emerged from the riverbank below. They were scraping, clawing sounds followed by an occasional small splash as bits and pieces of the riverbank fell into the water.

Finally, bleeding fingers could be seen pushing their way up through the grassy sod that covered the top of the bank. First, a small opening appeared, but the small hole became larger as two wide eyes stared up from the darkness.

The last of the tunneler's efforts was rewarded as a large portion of the bank top collapsed into the crocodile's home. Grasping at tree roots and grass, an exhausted Peter slowly pulled himself up from his watery grave.

The croc had cared little how his victim was stored until it rotted and was fit to eat. It was Peter's good fortune, however, that his head had entered the lair first and was pushed and shoved above the water line into the air pocket that the crocodile had carved out for his own breathing purposes. The beast had virtually left Peter sitting up in his underground cave with his head and shoulders leaning back against the riverbank, high and dry.

Of course, it was dark inside the lair when the young African regained consciousness and finally realized his situation. With only his upper body in the air pocket, he had the good sense to dig up through the riverbank rather than try to burrow a tunnel to the bottom of the river in which he sat.

After his escape, Peter walked down the river until he came to the only bridge in the area. Crossing over, he painfully limped home on his bruised and swollen ankle. Hurting and exhausted, he finally made it and was shocked to see a large crowd gathered on the lawn in front of his house.

As he got closer, he could see that the men appeared to be upset, and many of the women were crying. When the mournful group spotted him walking up the drive, several of them screamed and pulled back, thinking they were seeing a ghost.

Peter's mom heard the commotion and looked out from the front porch. She knew at once that this was not some kind of spirit she was seeing. Quickly, she ran to her son and held him tightly in her arms. Her boy had made it back from a most deadly picnic.

DID YOU KNOW?

- Crocodiles are one of the deadliest killers in Africa, second only to the hippo.
- Crocodiles can live to be more than 100 years old.
- Crocs are smart and observant. They watch for repeated patterns such as deer coming to drink at a certain water hole each day or women always washing clothes at the same spot on the river.
- Crocodiles usually eat fish, but they will take on anything they find in their waters.
- These water giants eat about every two weeks. They can remain submerged for about one hour.
- If you look in an adult crocodile's stomach, you will find about ten to fifteen pounds of stones and small rocks. Why? They swallow them to help them stay submerged.
- These reptiles have survived since the age of the dinosaurs. They are among the most adaptive creatures on earth.

ZIMBABWE—MYSTERY OF THE AGES

Alicia, look. There must be hundreds of them!" Annie exclaimed as we passed family after family of mongooses sitting on top of tall termite mounds near the road. The adults were about a foot long as they stood up on their back legs and watched as we drove by. They were furry and cuddly looking, like stuffed animals. "Aren't they cute?" she asked.

"They may be cute to us, but they scare the heck out of a snake. If you're lucky enough to have a family of mongooses living in your yard, you'll never have to worry about snakes. The cobra fears the mongoose more than he fears a lion," Dad said.

We had been driving for two days. Last night we had slept along the way at a government rest house, sort of a private little motel for people who do government work or teach at a government college like Dad does. We were on our way to the Zimbabwe ruins. It was once one of the greatest kingdoms in Africa, according to my father.

Annie and I were on spring break from school, and the college was also closed. The weather was beautiful after a long rainy season when it had been difficult to travel very much. Our entire family was beginning to feel shut in, sort of like cabin fever, as they call it. It was great being out on the road again.

Yesterday, darkness had fallen when a giraffe stepped out on the road in front of our car. Dad had slammed on the brakes in plenty of time, but we had just sat there astonished at the size of the animal in the headlights. "If he'd stand still, we could drive right under him," Dad had quipped. The tall animal's head must have been twenty feet in the air as he looked down at us. The large dark spots on his brownish coat stood out in the car's lights. His long stick-like legs were as tall as goal posts, and he looked almost prehistoric as he strolled across the road.

I guess I'd been dozing when Annie shouted, "There it is!" I sat up and looked up the hill at a giant fortress made of stone. Its big walls spread out over the hillside, like it was some kind of castle. We had been told that people had built Zimbabwe as a fortress to protect themselves from warring tribes and European invaders.

We were now driving in plateau country when we pulled into a small hotel where we would spend the night. Everybody was starving, so we washed up quickly and dashed right in for dinner. An elderly Shona man brought water and bread to our table and smiled warmly. In a few minutes he returned with vegetables and a large platter of assorted meats. "Bush meat, fresh and good," he said, smiling again.

We had traveled many roads in Africa, and we certainly knew about bush meat. Mom reached for a piece of chicken with her fork, which she knew was probably guinea fowl. Annie made the same choice while Dad and I speared our favorites. He took a long filet of snake meat, which he loves, while I went for the gopher.

Gopher is a big favorite with most Africans. They call these large rodents bush cutters because of the way they dig tunnels under growing plants. If one travels long enough in the wilderness, eventually you'll see small fires burning beside the road. Two or three Bantu women will be attending the coals while keeping a close eye on the barbecue meal. Generous portions of wild game will have been speared on short bamboo sticks and stuck in the earth around the fire pit.

If you ask what they are preparing, one of the women will always reply, "Bush meat," which will probably include gopher. Most American gophers are small, not much larger than a big rat. However, African gophers grow to the size of large rabbits, and they taste wonderful when cooked on an open fire. What do they taste like? you ask. Just like tender rabbit.

After dinner, Annie and I walked outside to stretch our legs. A large white moon gave the shimmering walls of the old ruins an eerie appearance. "This is a beautiful place in the moonlight, is it not?" a voice inquired. "My name is Joseph. I am one of the Zimbabwe guides. I would be honored to show you ladies the ancient city tomorrow, if you like."

Joseph was about twenty, Annie and I guessed later. He was very polite, and Dad was quick to agree that we'd learn a lot more if we had a guide.

The next morning our family met Joseph near the fortress. Mom and Dad had on jeans and hiking boots. Annie and I were wearing shorts and tops with our sneakers. Annie had a kerchief tied around her neck beneath her short, red hair.

"The Shonas are one of many Bantu tribes living in Africa, and these Bantu groups speak more than three hundred languages," our guide began. "Many years ago, a few of these tribes built large kingdoms like Kongo and Zimbabwe.

"In the early days, my people, the Shona, came to this high plateau country in search of good land to farm and to raise cattle. Not only were they looking for good land, but they also knew that this high country had few mosquitoes and tsetse flies. That meant our people could live healthier lives, free from malaria and sleeping sickness brought on by the dreaded tsetse fly. So, they moved up here, hundreds of years before the white Europeans discovered your country."

"When they built this place, why did they make the walls so high?" Annie asked. "And, I don't see any windows or doors. How did people get in and out?"

Joseph laughed. "These fortress walls are thirty feet high and twenty feet thick, but there are many doors and passageways. We are looking at the king's court, which is more than eight hundred feet long and has more than two hundred rooms for his wives and families. Come, I will show you how to get in."

Our guide led us to a place on the wall where several rope ladders hung down. "In the days of the Great Zimbabwe, a loud horn would sound if the city was attacked by bands of outlaws. People who lived in the small thatch huts outside the fortress would come running and climb rope ladders hanging down from the walls. Others who knew about the secret entrances in the rear would enter through those passageways."

Annie was the first up the rope ladder; then Mom followed. With everyone now atop the ancient wall we took in the sights. "Man, this is really neat up here," I said. "You can see forever. It would have been really hard for your enemies to sneak up on you here." From our vantage point we had sweeping views of the hillsides and the valleys below.

"Yes, this was quite a safe city. There were one or two small warring bands, but nothing serious. For years the Shona lived in peace and farmed the lands. Our people mined copper and iron from which they made spears and tools. But then, evil found its way into the city. Let's go inside."

We climbed down rope ladders, the same way that we had reached the top of the wall. Once inside, shadows played along the narrow corridors and passageways. We went down curved steps that had been carefully carved out of solid granite. "The workmanship is amazing. Your ancestors were excellent craftsmen, Joseph," Dad exclaimed.

"The first European explorers to come here claimed that no African tribe could have built this great granite city, that white men from Europe must have completed the work centuries ago. They refused to believe that Africans were this skilled, but scientists have since proven that it was indeed built by the Shonas."

"What brought on the downfall of the city, Joseph?" I asked.

"I said earlier that evil came into our city. What I meant was that one day someone discovered gold nuggets in the river. Soon more were found, and the Shona began mining the river for them. It was not long before Zimbabwe was a gold-rich city and the news traveled quickly. Craftsmen began designing and making gold jewelry and ornaments that were sold by merchants all over the land and down to the coast. Soon, small groups of Europeans, mostly Portuguese, began to visit the city."

"I'll bet that they were after the gold," Annie guessed.

"Yes, although we mined iron and copper, it was the gold that the foreigners craved. We had built our fortress city, and we were not about to give up what belonged to us without a fight. First the Portuguese soldiers came in small groups, then later by the hundreds."

"Did they finally conquer your granite city?" I asked.

"No, but they tried to do so for years. However, on their march from the coast to Zimbabwe, the mosquitoes brought down many with malaria, and the tsetse fly was also our ally. Try as they might, the Portuguese invaders never over-ran the Great Zimbabwe."

"What finally happened here?" Annie inquired.

"The invading armies had weakened our defenses so much that finally neighboring tribes began moving in, and the great Shona tribe lost its will to rule. The great fortress was no longer maintained, and it fell into ruin as you find it today."

Later, Dad paid Joseph for our excellent tour of what had once been the Great Zimbabwe. We had seen a wonderful chapter of African history and had been awed walking among the granite structures that had been so skillfully pieced together. The Shona had worked miracles here. And to think it had all been completed long before Columbus had set foot on American soil.

DID YOU KNOW?

- Zimbabwe means "houses of stone" in the Shona language.
- The African country of Zimbabwe took its name from the ancient fortress city that lies within its borders.
- The tsetse fly transmits a disease called nagana to cattle and a sleeping sickness to human beings.
- Scientists think the great city was built more than eight hundred years ago.
- The Shonas used about one million large granite stones to build the high fortress walls.
- At its peak, the Zimbabwe Kingdom controlled vast areas of southeast Africa.
- Thousands of abandoned gold mine shafts have been discovered in the hills surrounding the walled city.
- Shona craftsmen liked to make tools and utensils out of iron. At first they felt gold was too soft to be very useful.

HANSEL AND GRETEL

Most kids have heard the story of Hansel and Gretel. Remember, they got lost in the forest and were captured by the wicked witch? They were brother and sister, and so are the Hansel and Gretel we met in Africa; however, these two are lions.

Our friend Jim is what they call a game ranger in Africa. He lives in a small house on a remote game reserve hours away from the nearest town. Wild animals of every description roam these vast grasslands. It's Jim's job to protect them from illegal hunters called poachers. These small bands of men sneak onto the reserve to kill elephants and rhinos because their horns are valuable in some countries. Leopards and other cats are hunted for their coats.

One day Jim found two baby lion cubs wandering around without a mother. After a useless search, he brought them home to raise. With no mother, the two little ones would have perished in the wilderness.

The lion cubs were healthy and grew quickly. Jim named the boy cub Hansel and his sister was called Gretel, just like the two kids in the fairy tale.

After a year, each animal weighed more than two hundred pounds, twice the size of a police dog. Two years later, the felines had doubled their weight and were sleek and muscular. Hansel had a beautiful mane of black hair growing around his powerful neck.

Even though they were large, the two always thought they were just little cubs. To them Jim had always been their mommy and daddy, and they loved him dearly. Everywhere he went, they would follow. At night they'd climb up on the couch with him and fall asleep while he read. Jim would then sneak off to bed, hoping to have a little privacy. Later, when the big cats awoke, they headed straight for the bedroom and jumped up on the bed. There they slept with their dad nestled right between them.

The lions wanted to be with Jim all the time. They knew he started his day with a tour of the game reserve, and this ride was one of their favorite things to do. So, early each morning they'd trot outside and leap up on the roof of his pickup truck and wait. By being onboard, they knew Jim couldn't slip away without them.

Sometimes visitors came to the game reserve to watch and photograph the animals. They'd stay in one of the little mud and grass roofed huts that the Africans called rondolvos. Often Hansel and Gretel, who just loved people, would visit them and scare them to death. Sometimes Gretel would stand on her hind legs and put her front paws over the shoulders of some stranger and give him a big kiss on the face. Both lions liked to wrestle and romp, and sometimes their antics frightened the city folks.

Jim often wrestled with his lions, but he always took his shirt off first. If they felt the cloth on his back, they instinctively dug in their claws to hang on and Jim could be badly cut. Without his shirt, they felt his bare skin and always kept their claws tucked away so Jim wasn't harmed.

As time passed, people began to complain more and more about Hansel and Gretel and their playful games. Finally, after enough criticism, Jim made a tough decision. He put the two lions in the back of his truck and drove them far down the reserve to a nice spot near the river where there was plenty of food and water. While the animals investigated the area, Jim slipped away and drove back to his camp. He was certainly going to miss them, but people paid good money to see the reserve, and he didn't want them frightened.

The sister and brother quickly adjusted to being on their own and they thrived. Every week or so Jim would drive to the spot by the river and call out to them. Hansel and Gretel would hear his voice and come running, and all three would enjoy a playful romp on the grass.

As fall approached, a visitor from Germany arrived in Africa with plans to visit Jim's game reserve. The man rented a four-wheel, soft-top van in the city and set out for the wilderness. His main goal was to find lions and photograph them with his new video equipment.

He had only driven a few hours on reserve land when he suddenly slammed on the brakes. Standing in a grassy field near the road he saw the dream of his life. He couldn't believe his eyes. "Yes!" he shouted with joy as he watched the two magnificent lions standing near an acacia tree.

The German began filming the beautiful cats from inside the van. He was even more thrilled as the two felines began walking toward him, approaching the vehicle. His friends back home would be delighted to see such wonderful game photos, he thought.

However, the lions kept coming, getting a little too close. He stopped filming as his heart began to flutter and perspiration broke out on his brow. The man shrieked as both lions leaped up on the roof of the vehicle. In seconds the surprised cats also howled as they crashed through the cloth top, landing squarely on top of the tourist.

The photographer cried out as he fought for his life, pinned to the car seat by the two beasts. Frightened by their fall, Hansel and Gretel sprang from the vehicle and retreated quickly into the bush.

Badly shaken, but only scratched in the confusion, the German made his way to Jim's camp where he told his frightening story to other visitors gathered around the campfire. He spoke of how, just hours on the reserve, he had been attacked by two huge lions. Still filled with excitement, he explained how he had managed to fight off the two man-eaters who had fled toward the river.

Jim fought back a giggle as he listened to the German's tale. The next day he took a long drive and pulled off the dirt road at a familiar spot. He left his truck and walked toward the tall trees calling, "Hansel, Gretel." Down by the river's edge the lions spun around in the soft sand and raced toward the sound they heard. Jim had already removed his shirt, prepared to do battle, as the two sprang, knocking him to the ground.

For the next hour the threesome ran, hid, wrestled, and rested. When he was completely worn out Jim said, "Come on, kids, it's time to go home."

And home they went, happy to be together again. "The visitors will just have to put up with you two," Jim declared. "We're a family, and that's that."

DID YOU KNOW?

- Many countries in Africa have established wildlife reserves to protect animals.
- These areas are often patrolled by armed guards to keep out hunters.
- Much of Africa's wildlife has been lost to illegal hunters called poachers.
- Thousands of elephants and rhinos have been illegally killed by poachers who sell their tusks and horns to countries where they are ground up and used in various potions.
- Poachers also slip into game reserves to kill animals for their skins, which will be made into things such as rugs or handbags.
- Kruger National Park in South Africa is one of the largest game reserves on the African continent. Lions, elephants, and other game roam the nearly 8,000 square miles that includes six rivers.

FROM VILLAGES TO KINGDOMS

It had not been a particularly good day. Annie and I had gotten soaked on the way home from school. The storm came out of nowhere. First, there was distant thunder, followed by fierce black clouds that appeared in seconds. The scariest part is always the lightning that sometimes strikes the ground and runs along the road.

Annie yelled, "Let's run for the trees." Not far from the road several African women with babies tied to their backs stood under the protection of big palm trees. These are the same trees that provide palm fronds used for roofs on village huts.

The women welcomed us. "Mwapoleni Mukwai," they smiled while patting their chests gently with their right hands.

"Mwapoleni, Mulecosa?" Annie and I answered. The women had said hello to us, gesturing that they were happy to see us by patting their hearts. We said hello back to them but also asked how they were doing.

When storms like this come here, you find shelter wherever you can. Often, groups of Africans will run to our front porch for protection when caught out in this kind of weather. We don't mind because everybody does it. African or American, it's us against the storm.

When we got home we quickly shed our wet school uniforms. "Alicia, let's go over to Joko and Peter's house for a while."

"I can't, Annie. We're having a test in African history tomorrow, and I have to study my notes." I love history, but African history is complicated. There were so many ancient kingdoms, and village rules and customs are hard to understand.

I was studying my heart out when Mom knocked on my bedroom door. "We're having company for dinner in a few minutes, Alicia. You'd better get ready." When I joined the others, I found Mr. and Mrs. Lonwani sitting on our front room sofa. Peter and Joko's mom and dad are nice people, and it was good to see them.

We sat down for dinner. Then Annie and I listened to the adults talk. Mr. Lonwani teaches history at the college, and he's a really interesting person. "How are you girls doing in school?" he inquired.

"We're doing great, except for me," I replied. "I have an African history test tomorrow, and I think it's just too much for me. Ancient empires and tribal organization," I complained.

"It's true that Africa is a large continent, but just try to build a little map in your head. Picture things in your mind. For example, in the old days, there were great empires such as Ghana, Mali, and Songhai on the northwest coast. Just to the west of us was Kongo, and Zambesi was to the south.

"Remember, Alicia, Ghana was one of the earliest empires. Hundreds of years ago, it was a great trading center in west Africa. In your test tomorrow they might ask you about salt."

"Salt," I exclaimed. "Salt on a history test!"

"It may well be a question because the people of Ghana liked to cook with salt, and eating salt kept them healthy.

"Traders from the Middle East and Europe traveled across the Sahara Desert for hundreds of miles on camel trains to reach Ghana. They carried large blocks of salt with them because it was plentiful in the desert regions. The people of Ghana desperately needed that salt, so what did they have to trade with? Gold!"

"You've got to be kidding," I said. "They must have gotten tons of salt for a tiny bit of gold."

"Not true. Gold was plentiful in their empire, so they traded one pound of pure gold dust for one pound of salt."

"Wow," Annie jumped into the conversation. "That's insane!"

"Perhaps, but true. People have always been willing to trade for what is most precious to them. Camel trains carried the salt to west Africa and returned across the Sahara desert with gold. The people who ran those dangerous camel routes got very rich, if they lived. Many ran out of water or got lost and perished. It was a sixty-day, one-way trip across that blistering ocean of sand.

"It's hard to believe, but seven thousand years ago the Sahara desert was lush with forests and green savannas. Then, over the years, the climate changed dramatically, and it dried up like we find it today.

"So, Alicia, after the Ghana empire came to an end, it was followed by Mali, and later came the Songai empire. They were all great trading empires in their time, and they may well be on your test."

"And what were the other ones?" I asked.

"Kongo, which was our next-door neighbor, and Zimbabwe to the south. Unlike the others who traded across the Sahara, both Kongo and Zimbabwe traded with European countries like Portugal, from ports on the Atlantic and Indian Oceans. That's about it, Alicia. Not that complicated, is it?"

"This really helps, Mr. Lonwani. Thanks so much. But what about the organization and government of village life?"

"Most Africans who live south of the Sahara Desert, or sub-Sahara as we call it, live in villages both large and small. Sometimes many villages are ruled by the same chief and tribal council. The chief is the boss. He decides who is guilty or innocent of a crime and what the punishment should be. With the larger villages, he is also the commander and chief of the army, and he makes sure that his people are safe from crime and misdeeds.

"It's usually a male member of a large and very old family who becomes chief. Male members also serve on village councils. Chiefs can determine which tribes to trade with and when crops should be planted and cattle sold.

"In the old days, people made little cuts on their faces that healed and became permanent scars. These patterns of scars were different for every tribe. They became a sort of an identification that proved useful in recognizing your own people, or those from other tribes. Today, there are some tribes that still make tribal marks, but many have given up the custom.

"There, I hope this will help you, Alicia. You'll do well on your test."

Annie, the family jokester, gave everybody a laugh as our guests were leaving. "Mom, can I have a bag of gold dust please? I want to run down to the store and buy a little salt."

As for me, I remembered what Mr. Lonwani had said, and I did well on the test. As a thank you to him, I baked him a big batch of chocolate chip cookies.

DID YOU KNOW?

- The Islam religion found its way to the people of west Africa by way of the camel trains.
- Most of the traders that ran the camel trains to Ghana were Muslims.
- To show their respect when people came to see a tribal chief, they often came in bowing so their heads would be lower than his.
- African farmers often use fire to clear fields and keep unwanted growth away from their crops.
- Africans can have very large families that include many distant relatives. When these families grow to hundreds of people, they are called clans.

RAISING CHESTER

Annie and I will never forget the time that Dad took a trip to visit schools. Part of his assignment at the college was checking up on bush schools to see how they were doing. On his last stop he spent the night at a small hospital run by an American doctor. While they were touring the grounds, Dad and the doctor ducked into a tent that sheltered just two beds. "What do you think of this patient?" the physician asked.

Dad looked down at a small, furry baby. He was clad in a white diaper and was holding a baby bottle to his mouth. He was just so cute that he didn't look real, Dad later told us. Then the baby chimpanzee began to wiggle his little hairy arms, holding them up so he'd be picked up.

"He's about eight weeks old," the doctor said. "His mother was shot by poachers, but they couldn't find her baby. She had hidden the little guy under foliage."

By now the baby chimp had been picked up, and he had his arms wrapped around my father's neck. He rested his head on the warm neck and cuddled in tightly. "He's well now," the doctor continued. "All he needs is a good home. You have a couple of daughters, don't you?"

And that's all the urging it took. Dad drove carefully along the dangerous forest roads and crossed more than thirty-nine hand-built bridges before reaching the college. Throughout the trip he kept a close eye on the little passenger lying next to him on the seat.

Sometimes Dad brings us a present when he's been gone a few days. Annie and I ran out the front door when we heard the car pull into the driveway. "Hi, girls! Come see what I have for you!"

We opened the car door and there he was. We couldn't believe our eyes. The cutest baby we'd ever seen! He was so small and helpless that our hearts just went out to him. Now our lives would change dramatically because that was the day we began raising Chester.

In the coming weeks we took good care of our new baby. We named him Chester, and several times a day we fed him, changed his diaper, and played with him. Every night he curled up in bed between us. Soon he was running all over the house, anxious to play any game. He loved to climb and swing on the jungle gym and wrestle with us on the lawn. However, the game that Chester loved most was dress up.

We had a large wooden box filled with old clothes that we used to dress up when we and our friends put on plays for the neighborhood.

Chester was now a year old, and he liked to put on a dress and high-heeled shoes, then top off the outfit with a lady's straw hat. All made up, the three of us would parade around the house and yard, pretending that we were shopping in town. The following day we'd do the same thing, but always wearing different costumes.

One day we dressed Chester up like a baby again, diaper and all. We gave him a baby bottle and pushed him in a little carriage down the road. Some African women stopped to admire our baby and then let our shrieks of surprise seeing the hairy chimp grinning up at them. The little guy loved to scare them!

On another morning the three of us dressed up like African ladies wearing full-length wraparound dresses that almost touched the ground. We wore colorful head scarves, and each of us balanced a small basket of oranges on our head. Now dressed, we set off to find buyers for our fruit.

Africans are wonderful people, and they love nothing more than a good laugh. Crowds of them screamed with delight when they spotted our little trio with baskets balanced carefully on our heads, walking down the road. They were eager to buy our oranges, even from the lady with the grinning hairy face.

Chester continued to grow. By the time he was two years old, he was nearly four feet tall, very muscular, and strong. He could swing through the tallest trees in the yard and climb to the top of the jungle gym in seconds. We adored him and he loved us back.

Those were such fun times, with endless play on warm days. But then a problem began to develop. Chester was convinced we were his two mothers and that it was his job to protect us from strangers. That part we understood, but soon he began snarling at family friends who got too close to us. Our parents began to worry about where this sort of behavior might lead.

Christmas was just a few days away, so we went off shopping with Mom. While we were gone, Dad came home from another trip. We only heard about what happened next, but Dad said it went like this.

He parked his car in the driveway, unlocked the front door, and walked into the house. It was nearly dark, with the only light coming from the lighted Christmas tree. He tossed his keys on the side table while looking for signs of his family. Our Christmas tree stood at the other end of the long living room.

Suddenly the tree shook a little, then stopped. What was that? It wiggled again; then Santa Claus stepped out from behind the evergreen. He looked perfect in his red outfit with black boots, topped off by a red cap that was perched precariously on his head. Indeed it was Santa, but this one had large hairy arms.

Santa was pleased with his costume. He stood and gave Dad his best toothy smile as sort of a finishing touch to his modeling job. Then the big guy waited for the usual applause that came with a good dress-up act. But the expected clapping never came. Instead, Father broke out in uncontrollable laughter at the sight of Chester in all of his finery.

That did it! Chester shrieked in anger upon hearing the rude giggling. The chimp charged, but not on foot. He took to the trees like a good ape would. However, this time the trees happened to be the long drapes that covered the living room windows.

Leaping from his spot by the tree, he grasped the nearest window covering and began to swing down the long room toward Dad. At the end of a swing he would fly through the air, then catch the next window drape. One by one, he was bearing down on the person who had made fun of him. Letting go of the last covering, he landed next to Dad with a big thud.

The hairy face was still baring teeth, so Dad beat a hasty retreat out the front door. As he stood near the house, he remembered that he had left his keys inside. He realized he was now locked out of his own house.

Meanwhile, there was Chester looking out the window at him. The chimp had cooled down, and he was now engaged in a game of peekaboo. He grinned when he popped his face out from behind the curtain.

Dad tried opening a couple of locked windows to gain reentry into the house as Chester continued his game of peekaboo. Someone must have spotted Father's actions, because a patrol car with flashing red lights soon entered our driveway.

The two African police officers were polite, but they didn't believe my dad's story about an angry ape chasing him out of his own home. They became more suspicious when they heard the ape was dressed up like Santa Claus.

As the policemen questioned Dad, Chester would peek out the window when the officers weren't looking his way. When they turned to look at the house, he would duck behind the curtain again.

It was lucky that we got home from shopping when we did. We convinced the officers that Father was not a cat burglar and that there was indeed a crazy chimp in our house.

In spite of the incident, we all had a very merry Christmas, and Chester loved all of his gifts. The next year just flew by. Then it was time for us to return to our home in California. We had known for a long time that we couldn't take Chester with us, and the thought of leaving him behind was breaking our hearts.

There's a town nestled in the green, cool mountains about six hours' drive from here. It has a beautiful little zoo which has no cages, just small islands surrounded by waterways to keep the animals from straying.

It is there, on occasion, that visitors are treated to the sight of a graying chimpanzee pushing a baby carriage along the rock outcropping near his cave home on the hillside.

Friends write and tell about those special days when he emerges from his lair dragging a wooden box of old clothes behind him. During the holiday season he sometimes slips on a faded red costume and then searches in his box for the matching cap.

When dressed, Chester grins widely as the crowd cheers and children clap their hands with glee. We are so happy that our Chester loves his new home and his large family of admirers. At last he can play dress up whenever he pleases.

DID YOU KNOW?

- Chimpanzees in the forest live to be 40 to 50 years old.
- The male chimpanzee stands four to five feet tall and weighs 135–150 pounds.
- Chimpanzees make and use tools from twigs to catch ants and termites.
- They love to do hand-clapping and ground-stamping forms of dance in groups while they shout out their favorite sounds.
- Chimpanzees live in equatorial Africa. Baby chimps often stay near their mothers throughout their lives.
- Chimps often behave like people. When affectionate, they like to smile, hug, and kiss.

ABOUT THE AUTHORS

Les and Genny Nuckolls are both California natives with a love for traveling and writing.

Les first lived in Africa as a Fulbright Scholar assigned to teach at an African bush college near the Congo border. He continued living and traveling in Africa as a consultant to several Nigerian ministries for two years. During this time, he developed a deep appreciation and understanding of African family and cultural values. He and his two young daughters had some amazing experiences, many of which are chronicled in this book. Les finished off his overseas career as Superintendent of the Peace Corps Training Centers in the Caribbean.

After careers in education and administration, Les and Genny developed their passion for writing by working for several newspapers in Northern California. They have written their first book together to chronicle and celebrate the stories Les has always loved telling of his adventures in Africa.